SAVAGES

PAWNS OF PATIENCE

CASSIE JAMES

For Laura.
Thank you for cheering me on and loving these books
alongside me.

CONTENTS

This is a dead girl's crown.

Everyone is clapping. People who have barely looked in my direction since I showed up. People who didn't stand up for me when Jax humiliated me. Well, they're all looking at me now.

This crown, what it represents, it's a curse. It's power. And one of our classmates was willing to kill for it. Why aren't people more upset? They're all looking at me like this makes sense, but none of this makes sense to me. I glance up just to be sure there's no pig's blood waiting for me in the rafters.

"Juliet?" Patrick offers me his hand. "We're supposed to dance now."

I let him guide me down the steps of the small stage, out onto the floor in the middle of the gathering crowd. I thought they only did the first dance thing in movies. Patrick pulls me close, one hand settling around my waist as he keeps my hand clasped tight in the other. I bury my face against him as he effortlessly guides me across the floor.

"You make a good Prom King," I tell him, tilting my face up just slightly. "I really half-expected it would be Jax." He seems to get everything else handed to him—why not this, too?

Patrick scoffs. "People might let Jax get away with a lot because of who his dad is, but that doesn't mean they have to like him. All the shit he's been doing to you hasn't gone unnoticed, babe." I don't say anything, but it's funny how quick he is to forget the times when he was the one being the asshole. "You make a good Queen," he adds, holding me a little tighter as I bite back a laugh.

"No, I didn't earn this crown."

"Like hell you didn't," a voice interrupts. I look over Patrick's shoulder, pulling away slightly to get a better look. Jax's eyes—so dark and haunted—look at me like I'm the only thing he sees in the room.

"Juliet?" I jolt out of my chair, my heart kicking into overdrive. "Sorry, I didn't mean to startle you."

Smith is standing in the doorway with his hands tucked in his front pockets. As I stand up to go to him, I let out a long yawn. With a quick glance, I see that Pearl is still asleep, so I beckon for Smith to follow me out into the hall, pulling the door closed behind us. Despite the fact that this is easily the nicest hospital I've ever seen in real life, the stringent smell of cleaner still assaults my nose out here. Pearl bullied one of the nurses into finding her an air freshener in the middle of the night, so her room smells more like roses than hospital.

"How is she?" Smith asks, real concern on his face. I work my jaw back and forth, trying to decide how to answer that. Pearl is Pearl—dying doesn't seem to be changing that. Despite the doctors' concerns about the fall she took, she was still lucid all night. Lucid enough to warn me that she didn't want me sharing details of her condition. The paranoia was in full swing.

Knowing we can't stand here in silence forever, I cave and tell him, "The doctors are worried. They don't want her to go home, they want her to go to a long-term care place."

"If that's what they think is best—"

I shake my head hard, cutting him off. "No. Absolutely not." The idea of sending her into one of those sterile, lifeless places makes me sick to my stomach. I haven't broached the subject with Pearl herself, yet, but I'm sure she'll agree. She's guarded Lexington Estate with her life, and that's the only place I'm taking her when she leaves here.

Regardless of how not warm and fuzzy the two of us are together, Pearl is family, and family is supposed to take care of family. I didn't have that growing up, so there's no way in hell I'm giving it up now. For all the flaws in our relationship, Pearl let me come home. Now, I want to do the same for her.

Smith's easygoing expression falters as I blink

out a few stray tears. This has all been too much. Twelve hours ago, I was wearing a prom dress and trying to figure out how the hell I ended up becoming the stand-in Prom Queen. Now, I'm standing in the middle of a hospital in oversized sweatpants and a gift shop t-shirt that I got last night from one of the nurses that took pity on me. I'm just so, so tired of feeling like I can never quite get my footing here.

"Hey, don't do that." Smith grabs me around the waist to tug me close to him, letting me bury my face in his chest. This is starting to become a habit; it's the same thing I did last night with Patrick.

"This sucks." The words come out muffled, but he must get the gist of it, because he strokes my back and shushes me.

"It's gonna be alright, Jules." His voice cracks, which just breaks my heart all over again. I hate that my hurt is hurting him, too. "Whatever you want to do, I'll help you figure it out." He pauses for a moment before he adds, "We all will."

I fist his shirt in my hand, struggling to hold back a wave of fresh tears threatening to come. Why does he have to be the sweetest boy in the whole world? It's crazy this is the same guy who grabbed me so hard I bruised and blew pot in my face the first few times we met. I take several deep, calming breaths before I can talk again.

I pull back and look in those damn baby blues of his. "I told you all not to come," I remind him. That was the first thing I told them last night when Headmaster Dupont interrupted our prom to tell me Pearl had fallen and was on her way to the hospital.

"Last night, I figured you were right because I'd be more in the way than anything, but I couldn't wait any longer. I wanted to check on you." He kisses my temple.

"Thank you." I still have a fistful of his shirt, so I use it to pull him in, planting a long kiss on his lips. It's a hospital, I'm not interested in getting too frisky, but when his lips part I indulge for a minute. Pulling away only when I hear squeaking footsteps sound like they're heading our way.

I step away from him just in time to greet the same nurse who brought me clothes last night. Her eyes dart between Smith and I, a soft smile crossing over her face as she clearly takes stock in what was happening. She stops a couple feet away from us, a polite distance away but still close enough to talk without anyone else overhearing. Not that there's really an abundance of foot traffic. Add it to the list of differences between my old life and my new; Patience's closest hospital is a hell of a lot nicer than anything within at least an hour of Nikon Park.

"Sorry to interrupt," the nurse says with a coy smile. "But my shift is ending and I wanted to check in one last time before I go."

"Everything is good, thank you." I lean into Smith, the gesture so natural I barely notice I'm doing it. The nurse notices, though, the skin around her eyes crinkling as she looks at us with something like relief.

"Good. I'm glad you finally have some company. The doctor should be coming around soon, he was hoping to see your aunt first thing." *Yeah, because she pitched a bitch fit last night when she had to wait more than thirty minutes for the on-call doctor to make it to her.*

At least the nurse's reaction to seeing me with Smith makes more sense now. She's hoping I won't be alone when the doctor comes around this time. I don't need to correct her assumption, but there's no way Smith can be here for that. Pearl would climb right out of that hospital bed and wring my neck if she knew a *Harrington* might hear about how sick she is.

"Great. Thank you. And thank you again for the clothes, too." God, how many freaking times am I going to thank this woman?

"No problem, sweetie. I'll just pop in and check on Pearl again, then be on my way." She tells us goodbye and quietly lets herself into my great aunt's room. I'm sure Pearl will be wondering where I disappeared to, but I'm not ready to go back in there. Not just yet.

Smith nods toward the elevator. "Can I buy you a quick coffee? We can go right downstairs to the cafeteria," he adds when I tense up.

"A coffee sounds good," I admit, nodding now that I know he's not asking me to go further than an elevator ride away. I slept like crap last night. I'm sure I'll need coffee to get through this day, even if it is just a weak cup from a hospital cafeteria. Beggars can't be choosers.

We take a quiet trip downstairs where we drink coffee in silence, sitting at a table by the window so I can look out at the rest of the world. It's funny how last night, when I got the news about Pearl, my whole world seemed to stop, but everyone else kept moving. There was no one else to call, and that makes me sad. It makes me think about how if I hadn't ended up in Patience, Pearl would be completely alone. She has no other family and no friends from what I can tell. The only person she ever really talks about is Hollis, and he's been gone for a decade. What a lonely life to have lived.

It's not until we're on our way back up that I catch Smith looking at me intently. He thinks I don't notice because I'm not facing him, but I can see his reflection in the elevator walls.

"What?" I ask, turning to look at him head-on.

"Juliet." He wraps an arm around my waist and drags me in so that we're chest to chest. "I—" Whatever he was about to say gets cut short as the elevator doors open one floor before ours and a couple steps on. They step to the far side of the elevator, leaving as much room between us as they can in such a tight space.

"You, what?" I try to ask, but Smith shakes his head, warily eyeing the other people. I guess whatever he was going to say couldn't have been too important, then.

He puts his hand on my lower back as we step off on the next floor. It feels like someone is tying weights to my ankles the closer we get to Pearl's room. I wish I didn't have to go back in there, but I know I do. We stop just outside the view of her open doorway to say our goodbyes.

And by *say our goodbyes*, I definitely mean kissing. So much kissing. More kissing than is probably appropriate for the middle of a hospital. I let myself just enjoy the moment, his tongue swiping mine carefully as if I'm fragile, and right now maybe I am. When Smith pulls away—he pulls away before I do—I'm half-tempted to drag him back to me. He wraps his arms around me and squeezes me tight, offering me one last moment of comfort.

"Will you please call me if you need anything?" he asks when he pulls away.

I nod, even though I know I won't. As happy as I am that Smith came, I don't want to burden anyone.

"Juliet," he says my name in a warning growl. It's like he read my mind. "I'm serious."

"Okay," I cave, hoping like hell that I just won't need anything. Smith, for someone that seemed so desperate to play the role of a bad boy when I met him, is actually a closet sweetheart.

Speaking of sweethearts… "Did you get ahold of Ace?" I ask. He left early last night before the call about Pearl came in. Something about a newborn horse that I didn't quite understand. Until Patrick explained it to me last night, I hadn't even known that Ace's family owned a lucrative horse farm on the outskirts of Patience. I can't remember ever even seeing a horse in real life, but apparently the Van Dorens own millions of dollars worth of them—which is pretty much unfathomable to me.

"Jax went by there last night to tell him in between Prom and Allie's after-party."

My shoulders go tense. Of all the people that could have gone by there, why did it have to be the one person I don't trust in the least? Jax blackmailed Ace before, so I'm sure he wasn't Ace's first choice for news delivery either. *Dammit.*

"What?" Smith asks, noticing my unease.

"Could you maybe just double-check that Ace knows?" The unspoken part of my sentence hangs in the air between us. I know Jax is Smith's friend, but he has to realize that Jax has been nothing but nasty to me since I showed up. It isn't such a stretch for me to not quite trust him.

"I know you think Jax is always the bad guy but—"

"Please," I interrupt. "Just double-check. I don't want to have this argument with you again. Not here and not right now." It's the same argument we keep coming back to time and again. Smith's loyalty is always with Jax, and for some reason he thinks I should trust him too. Even when Jax has given me every reason to believe he doesn't have my best interests at heart.

"I will. Of course I will." He leans in for a last kiss, a short peck that doesn't last nearly long enough. But it's time for Smith to go.

I watch him leave, waving one last time as he disappears into an elevator at the end of the hall. After one more minute to compose myself again, I step into Pearl's room. I'm surprised to find her sitting up and completely alert. Based on the look in her eyes, I'm not so sure I got away with Smith being here after all.

"With all the boys coming around trying to sniff under your tail the last few months, I'd really hoped that Harrington boy wouldn't come out on top." She heaves a deep sigh as I gawk at her ashen face. *Did she seriously just imply that my guys are dogs trying to sniff my ass? Good god, where has her filter gone?*

"I like Smith," I say carefully. "And I like the other boys, too."

Pearl gives me a knowing look. "Yes, I'm sure any warm-blooded young woman would. You know, I had more than one boyfriend at a time when I was your age."

"Really?" Picturing Pearl with even one boyfriend feels like a stretch, but there's nothing to suggest she's saying it to make a dig at me. I thought my arrangement with the guys was going largely unnoticed, especially considering we haven't worked the kinks out—no pun intended—but apparently Pearl has caught on to more than I realized.

"And a girlfriend, too," she says with a nod, looking awfully damn proud of herself when I choke on my own spit. Now she's definitely got my full attention.

"What happened?"

"Life." She heaves another one of her long sighs. "The world was even crueler then than it is now. My lady love couldn't handle the heat and then jealousy started to tear at my two young men until they both jumped out of the frying pan as well."

My heart aches for her, trying to picture a young Pearl heartbroken not once, but three times, and all within that one relationship. Is that the inevitable end for me too? By not wanting to choose between the boys who have captured my heart, am I ultimately destined to lose all of them? The thought makes my heart pound harder and sweat break out along my hairline. The last thing I want is to fall for these guys only to lose them.

I already lost Jake. I don't want to lose anyone else.

"Stay in Patience, Juliet." Pearl is starting to blink sleepily now. I don't know that she'll be able to stay awake much longer. Her head has already started to sink back against her pillow.

"I'm not going anywhere, I'm right here," I reassure her.

She shakes her head slightly. "Stay in Patience

because you're a queen here. They'll let you make the rules. It can't be guaranteed elsewhere." I smile and nod, trying to offer some comfort to her by agreeing with her. If I'm being honest, I have no idea what she's talking about. I'm assuming she means I'm a Prom Queen here, but I think she's grossly overestimating how much power that affords me to be openly unconventional.

Pearl dozes for a while as I sit quietly by her bedside, still turning her words over in my head. It's strange she wouldn't warn me away from dating more than one person considering how her own relationships turned out. She didn't give me as much shit about Smith as I expected either, though to be fair she still seems a little delirious. And maybe that's just the explanation for all of it. She's not in her right mind. Hell, for all I know she completely made up the little story about dating multiple people.

She's on pain medication because the fall she took twisted her arm up pretty bad. That's probably just making her a little unstable in the mind. I need to get her out of here, get her back home where she can get her wits about her again. A concept which proves to be more difficult than I planned when the doctor shows up.

"There are some great facilities, with resources far beyond what you're able to offer her at home." I can tell from his voice that he's getting exasperated with me, but I don't back down.

"As I told you last night, I'm taking her home. Lexington Estate has been her home her whole life. No one gets to steal that from her now." Especially not when it means going to some sterile place that's basically just a hospital with a different name. I don't care how nice the long-term care facilities are, they're still just glorified hospitals. Pearl is *not* spending the end of her life in a hospital. Not on my watch.

Pearl, who's barely been awake through all of this, reaches out to pat my hand with hers. "It's okay, Juliet. I can go to the death hotel."

I shoot the doctor a look as his expression turns uncomfortable. *See?* I want to say. She's calling the place a death hotel for fuck's sake. I am not under any circumstances dropping my sole living family member off at a death hotel. I'd sooner take her out to sea and give her a Viking funeral than submit her to that fate.

"What is the point," I start, taking a deep breath when my voice starts to crack. I try again, "What is the point in having more money than any sane person should ever be allowed to hoard if we don't use some of it for things that matter? Things like this. I'm more than capable of paying for full-time care for Pearl *at home* for as long as she needs it. Which is hopefully still a hell of a long time. So, if you could just point me in the right direction for that—that's the only resource I need from you. No more pamphlets for these places." I shove the long-term care placement pamphlets back at him, which he reluctantly takes.

"When we discussed the options—"

"You're fired." My voice is deadpan as the doctor immediately started spluttering. I completely ignore him now as I push the call button on Pearl's bed. When a nurse picks up the intercom, I ask her, "Is there another doctor available?"

She pauses for a split second before confirming that there is. "Dr. Yorke is here today. He's with another patient right now but he should be finishing up."

"Perfect. Could you send him our way when he's done? We're in need of a second opinion." I look at the now fired doctor with a smug look as the nurse tells me it won't be a problem. If this guy isn't going to listen, maybe the next one will. I'm done playing these stupid games that seem more like a power trip than actual medical advice. What the hell can anyone really do that an obscene amount of money can't replicate at home?

As the doctor closes the door a little too hard behind him, Pearl grins at me. "It's good to see you finally growing into things."

"What do you mean?"

"No one pushes a Lexington around," she says softly, already drifting back to sleep. *Now there's a family trait I can get behind.*

2

Dr. Yorke turns out to be an absolute godsend, and within days Pearl is settled at home in a new state-of-the-art hospital bed that had to be flown halfway across the country on a private plane to get here on time. Every check I sign makes me cringe, but I remind myself that this is barely a drop in the pan that I'm spending. I could live ten lifetimes and not even make a dent in my new finances. It's all just a little overwhelming.

I put the guys off as long as I can, not wanting to anger Pearl by filling the house with people. They can only be held off for so long though, so when the doorbell rings, I'm not exactly surprised that it's the guys. Well, okay, maybe I'm a little surprised to see Jax with them.

Seeing them, it's enough to make my whole body sag with emotion. I reach out blindly, not even quite sure who I'm reaching for, and end up pulling Patrick, Ace, and Smith into a group hug. Jax, who's standing a couple feet off from the group doesn't participate, but he catches my eye between Smith and Ace's shoulders. He's staring at me hard too, the same way he did when he interrupted my dance with Patrick at prom.

It makes me uncomfortable enough that I cut the embrace short and pull away, smiling to cover up the weird feelings suddenly flowing through me. *Why does he keep looking at me like that?*

Patrick is the first to talk. "I know you said you didn't want us to come," he starts, but I shake my head before he finishes making excuses for showing up unannounced.

"I'm glad you're all here," I tell him honestly. I didn't realize how much I needed them until I saw them standing in my doorway. My eyes cut over to Jax again, looking for a reaction, but he gives me nothing but his stare. My words are the truth. I'm glad they're *all* here, even Jax for some strange reason. I can't tell by looking at him if it matters that I'm including him or not. He looks pretty unfazed by all this, but hell, he's the one that chose to show up. Realizing I'm still standing in the doorway gawking at them, I step back and wave them inside.

"We meant to take turns so we wouldn't over-whelm you," Patrick tells me, turning his eyes down-ward as he shrugs. "But then no one could agree who would get to come first. I hope it's okay, we just didn't want to cause an issue. This way we're all seeing you at the same time."

I spare a quick glance at Smith, but he shakes his head discreetly. He doesn't want the others to know he's already seen me. Once at the hospital, and one quick time here when I first brought Pearl home.

It's sweet really, seeing him try to spare the other guys' feelings. Particularly Patrick, whose little display of jealousy at Prom I definitely haven't forgotten.

"Pearl's in the formal room. She's been pretty lucid today, but if you guys aren't comfortable going in there, we can hang out in the kitchen for a few?" I've stuck pretty close to Pearl's side, much to her annoyance. We have several full-time nurses rotating shifts that don't even watch her as closely as I do. I keep telling her I can't help it, it makes me anxious to leave her by herself with nothing to do and no company. She wouldn't even let me put a TV in there for her.

"I've got my memories to keep me company, Juliet," she'd said. And apparently that's really all she wants because I can't even get her to pick up a book. She did let me pull the family photos out again to look through. I guess those go along with her memories though, so that makes sense.

Ace is the first to take a step, but instead of pointing his feet towards the kitchen, he moves solidly towards where Pearl is. I hope like hell she won't be mad that they're here, but it's actually a relief when all the guys follow suit, letting me go back to Pearl instead of entertaining them in another room.

"Well, my my." Pearl pushes the button on her bed that allows her to sit up straighter. "If I'd known I was going to get so many handsome young visitors, I would have started dying a lot sooner."

The guys shoot each other uncomfortable looks, wholly unfamiliar with Pearl's new lack of polite, old lady filtering. All except Jax, who snorts out a laugh.

Pearl grins at him, pleased to see someone enjoying her dark little joke. She reaches a hand out to him, and he indulges her by going to her bedside. She looks awestruck as she stares up at him. "If only Hollis were here. He'd be as pleased as a dog with two tails to see Jax Woods back in this house." Her eyes cut over to me. "The two of you used to be inseparable. The nannies had to put you down for naps together, that's how obsessed the two of you were with each other. Just babies, but already so connected."

I don't bother reminding her that she's told me that story before. Twice now, actually. Let her have her moment, even if it does make my cheeks flush with embarrassment to hear her describe us that way.

"*So connected,*" Patrick mocks under his breath,

but Smith shoots him a sharp look before I can say anything.

Pearl looks past Jax now, taking her time looking over each of the other guys. "You're a large bunch aren't you?" she says. She points a long finger at Ace, pointing first at his face but then letting her finger trail down until she's pointing directly at his crotch. "Especially you."

I gasp, jumping forward to stop her before this goes any further. "Kitchen!" I take a deep breath. "We're going to the kitchen. I'll make the boys say bye before they leave." I waste no time shoving them out of the room before Pearl can say anything else to leave me permanently scarred.

Ace drags his feet, staying back with me a little as the others surge forward. They've been in this house more than enough times to know where they're going. Ace's face might actually be redder than mine I realize when I take a good look at him. Then, all on their own, my eyes drop to his crotch.

"Jesus," he groans, putting his hands down as if to cover himself. "Stop staring, Juliet. Before I embarrass myself."

Even with him trying to cover himself with his hands, I can see the way his jeans struggle to contain him. *Ace is getting hard just from me looking.* And shit, I'm still staring. My self-control is clearly functioning at a zero right now. Damn though, Pearl wasn't wrong. I'm honestly a little terrified to picture what Ace has in his pants.

"Dammit, Juliet, stop it." My mouth falls open, fully prepared to protest that I'm not doing anything. "I can still feel you thinking about it," he tells me, his flush spreading further down his neck.

Patrick pokes his head out at the end of the hall, his eyes narrowing at how close Ace and I are standing. "Are the two of you coming?"

"Yeah," I answer, annoyance tinging my voice. I can already tell that I'm going to have to have another talk with Patrick. I know I told him I wouldn't give up on him, but I need to know this isn't how it's always going to be. I don't want to walk on eggshells with Ace or Smith just because Patrick can't handle it. What we're doing, this arrangement, it can't work with that toxicity hanging over our heads.

I start to go but Ace touches my arm. "Cut him a little bit of slack. He's used to always being on top and never having to share anything."

Ace's words make me soften. He's still integrating into things, merging with the little group I've created even though we never really had a conversation about what it is we're doing. If Ace can give Patrick breathing room to adjust, then I need to remember that I can too. That thought does bring up another important point though.

"We never really talked about things with us. I appreciate you going to prom with me after my little faux pas with Patrick and Smith, but beyond that, I never really asked if you wanted to do this."

He squints at me. "What is *this* exactly?"

Now that I've brought it up, I sort of wish I hadn't. I'm giving him the chance to ask for an out, even though that's the last thing in the world I want. He deserves that, I remind myself. This won't work if I'm strong-arming anyone into something they're not comfortable with.

"I like you." I take a deep breath that does nothing to steady me. "And I like Smith. And I like Patrick. Maybe it's selfish or not fair to want you all, but I really don't want to choose. Not now. Maybe not ever."

"I haven't asked you to," he reminds me with a hard look.

"I know. I just don't want you to feel like you slipped into a relationship that you don't want just because we got so close after what happened over the break..." I trail off, remembering what a shit show all of that was. And all of it still unresolved, too. Cece. My not-mom. Hollis. I can't stomach thinking about any of that now.

"I think I've learned my lesson about saying no to things I don't want." He grabs me by the hand as he steps closer, kissing me right on the edge of my mouth. It's not nearly enough, but for now it has to be, since my other two boyfriends are standing in the next room waiting for us. *How on earth did I ever get myself into this?*

"What about Jax?" Ace asks.

That makes me frown. "What about him?"

"Where does he fit into all of this?"

"He doesn't." I glance back toward the kitchen, making sure no one is nearby eavesdropping. "I don't even know why he's here."

Ace studies me so closely that I start to worry I said something wrong. Just when I'm about to ask, he lets out a bark of laughter that nearly makes me jump right out of my skin. He drops his hands on my shoulders and offers me an apologetic frown.

"Sorry." He calms himself. "I just... He's here for *you*. Do you really not get that?" I just stare blankly at him. I know Jax isn't here *for me*, because the only person he does anything for is himself. I tell Ace as much, and he barks out another laugh. "I think you're in for a rude awakening, Juliet."

"Why?"

He shakes his head and slides one arm across my shoulders as he tugs me forward, toward the kitchen. "Nuh-uh. I'm not getting involved. Woods can figure this one out all by himself for once."

I'm not a complete idiot. I get what Ace is insinuating, that Jax likes me—in whatever way that demon spawn is capable of liking anyone. But even if he's right, and this isn't some new, elaborate scheme to humiliate me, I'm not sure how interested I am. Not only would I be adding a new boy to the mix, but it would be someone that I have insane physical chemistry with and not much else. My guys? They've made me feel cared for and comforted, whereas Jax has only ever made me feel cheap, used, and unwelcome.

Neither Ace nor I say anything else about it. He keeps his arm slung over me as we enter the kitchen, the other three guys turning to stare. No one looks mad, so that's a good start.

Ace lets go of me so I can sidle up onto a stool at the island. Jax is standing on the other side, his eyes still focused on me just like before. It's really starting to get to be too much at this point.

"Please, for the love of all that is holy, stop staring at me like that," I finally snap.

Without a word, he storms around the island and right out of the kitchen. A few seconds later, there's the distinct sound of the front door slamming. I cross my arms on the counter in front of me and drop my head down on them, a headache starting to pulse between my eyes. How is it that Jax spends months being an asshole to me, and yet I snap at him one time and I'm the one that ends up feeling guilty?

Because you know better and he doesn't.

Raising my head, I look at Smith to say, "Will you please check on him?"

Relief floods his face as he nods. I'm sure he was already trying to figure out how to excuse himself. I can't say I understand the bond between the two of them, but if Smith isn't making me choose, then I guess I need to start realizing that I can't ask him to either. And Jax? Whatever the hell is going on with him right now, I'm sure he could use a friend.

"How about a walk out back?" I look back and forth between Patrick and Ace, who both nod easily. I really need the fresh air. Maybe if I can somehow get enough of it, I'll stop feeling like I'm spending all my time suffocating. As I listen to the front door close again, I can't help but think that then again, maybe I won't.

3

I lose track of the days as summer drags on; the sunlight pouring in through the front windows as Pearl refuses to let me close the curtains even partway. It makes the room unbearably hot, to the point that we've got six different fans in here now, each of them pointing a different direction to try to keep the cool air flowing. It's not even that hot outside really, the huge front windows just happen to turn this room into an overexposed greenhouse. I offered to move Pearl to a different room, but she didn't want that, either.

She keeps giving me shit for not enjoying my summer, but that's one argument I haven't let her win. I'll have plenty more summers, but I won't have another one with her.

It's another day of her begging me to get out of the house when someone pounds on the front door. The nurse, Jan—a robust woman who talks too fast and spends all day fussing over me as much as Pearl —stands up to get it, but I gesture for her to sit back down.

"I can get it," I reassure her.

Answering the door isn't really part of her job, and even though we're paying her a small fortune to mostly just hangout drinking our coffee, I still don't want to take advantage of her. Of all the nurses, Jan is admittedly my favorite. Probably because she feels like a grandmother, something I've never had.

We weren't expecting anyone, but the face that greets me when I open the door is probably the literal last person I ever would have guessed.

"Governor?" I do a weird sort of head nod that probably looks half like I was trying to bow to him. I feel totally ridiculous, but I never expected to be greeting our state governor at the door in my daisy dukes.

He gives me a withering look and a quick once over. Yeah, doesn't look like he's such a fan of the daisy dukes. I should probably be more offended by how dismissively he looks at me, but honestly, I'm just relieved when he doesn't ogle me the way those old men at the country club did that time. That would have been way worse than the cutting way he's looking at me.

"I'm here to see Pearl," he announces, not bothering to greet me in any way. He shifts slightly, moving just enough that I see the familiar dark eyes of the person standing behind him. Jax. Noticing my look, the governor adds, "I'm not sure why my son decided to join me, if that's what you're wondering. You'll have to ask him that."

Jax glares at his father's back, his jaw clenching. If it were anyone else, the expression would scream anger, but Jax actually looks... embarrassed. Jax Woods is embarrassed. *Interesting.*

"Come on in, sir." I step aside so the governor can enter. I'm not particularly fond of the man based on our limited interactions so far, but I'm pretty sure you can't just say *thanks but no thanks* when a man like that comes to visit.

A couple of men in suits trickle in behind him. I hadn't even noticed them before, probably because I was so shocked to see Jax back here. After the last time he stormed out, there hasn't been any sign of him. The other guys have popped in to visit for short periods, but Jax hasn't made any more appearances —which is really for the best, probably. He's here now though.

He walks in behind security, shoving me out of the way so he can be the one to close the door for some reason. I narrowly avoid bouncing off the wall when he pushes me out of his way. *Jerk.*

"I'd like to speak to Pearl. Alone." I look over to see that the governor's talking to Jan. My eyes narrow as I take a step forward, fully prepared to berate him for talking to my stand-in grandma like that.

Jax puts a hand out to stop me. "We've met Jan

before. Dad hired her to sit with my mom for a few weeks the last time she was battling a pill problem. She knows how he is; she won't take it personally."

He sounds so sincere about it that I back off. I still don't like it, but Jax is right, Jan doesn't look the least bit offended as she strolls out of the room, knitting in hand, and tells me I can find her in the library when Pearl's ready for her again.

Governor Woods gives his security guys instructions to stay out of the room too, which surprises me. They took up a stance right by the doorway as the governor pointedly closes the door to the room between us. Now, it's just me, Jax, and some rando security guys whose meaty thighs look like the size of almost my whole body. I shudder. They're super intimidating.

Jax, if he notices, doesn't comment. Mostly because he's too busy grabbing my arm and hauling me up the steps.

"What are you doing?" I grit out as I try desperately to dig my bare feet into the ground. It's not any use, Jax is a man on a mission right now and I'm just along for the ride. Until I realize he's bee-lining straight for my bedroom.

"Stop." I grab onto the doorframe as he tries to push me into the room. "Jax, stop!"

That finally gets his attention. "Stop yelling," he hisses, eyes darting back toward the stairs. My eyes widen as I look at him, wondering if he's for real. He's dragging me to my bedroom, which is obviously really freaking me out, but he's worried my being loud will attract attention? Uh, I hope it fucking *does*.

"Let go of me," I try again, though this time my voice sounds downright panicked. I'm not even that angry, just scared at this point.

Jax lets go of me so fast it's like I'm suddenly on fire and he's scared of getting burnt. He stares at me like I'm some foreign object, instead of the girl he just manhandled through half the house. I don't dare let go of the doorframe, worried he's only trying to get me to let my guard down now.

"I told you last time not to ever touch me again," I remind him, watching his eyes flash as I bring up the last time he got too rough with me.

"I wouldn't have to drag your ass around if you would just do what I ask." He crosses his arms as he leans back against the wall. He's still within grabbing distance, but he looks slightly less threatening now with his relaxed posture. I loosen my grip just slightly—enough that my fingers stop cramping from holding on too tight.

"You didn't ask me to do anything! You just started dragging me up here like a caveman." I shake my head, truly baffled by the nerve of him.

"Because I knew you wouldn't listen to me," he snarks back.

I can't help myself. Really, I can't. I let go of the wood of the doorframe and just fucking hit the hell out of him. In the stomach, in the arm, anywhere I can reach really. I hit him until some of the sudden rage is gone and I'm panting from the effort.

"Are you done now?" he asks, not even the least bit fazed.

I glare at him and hit him one more good time in the gut. He winces, much to my glee. At least I got one good hit in, even though he immediately straightens back up and acts like that one didn't bother him either. Asshole.

"Why did you make me think you didn't care about Kathryn's death?" I blurt out. This is so not the right time to be having this conversation, but it's a question that's been weighing on me for weeks.

"Because I don't."

"But your dad was the one that put the pressure on the police department to solve the case as quickly as they did. Didn't you have something to do with that?" I can't imagine Governor Woods doing anything like that on his own. Not after he tried to keep everything quietly swept under the rug and encouraged everyone not to talk.

"Yeah, only because that's what you wanted." He frowns. "Wasn't it?"

"Yeah," I say slowly. "That's what any decent human being should want. No one's parents or friends should have to go without answers after something like that. They deserved to know."

"I'm not going to pretend I give a shit about the Lassiters or Kathryn's frenemies, Juliet. I made that happen because it was what you asked me for.

Because you made that goddamn comment about how it could have been anyone, and then I couldn't stop picturing that it could have been you."

There's a level of emotion in his voice that makes me uncomfortable, mostly because I absolutely never hear him talk like that. This is why Smith told me to talk to Jax when he told me what the Governor had done. He already knew Jax had done it for me. He wanted Jax to have to tell me himself.

I think back to what it was Ace said when I first brought Pearl home. *"He's here for you. Do you really not get that?"* I'd doubted the truth of it at the time, but what if it's not a scheme? What if Jax has feelings and this is the only way this asshole knows how to show it? Is that what everyone but me has already seen? But god, it's hard to forget what an asshole Jax has been. The way he's humiliated me and tried to run me off. It seems like a lot of cruelty to throw at someone just to turn around and decide you care for them. Enough to manipulate a whole police investigation.

"I don't know what you want me to say," I admit, too many negative emotions still swirling inside of me to play nice with him. "You did something you should have done in the first place, so I'm not exactly ready to hand you a blue ribbon for being a decent person."

Anger flashes in his eyes. "The police department couldn't get the job done. I fucked Cece, all so I could get ahold of her phone and prove her alibi was bullshit. She coached that freshman into saying they hooked up when they didn't. I got that proof for them. I handed them the solution to that case."

That makes so much damn sense and answers so many questions for me. Like why on earth Jax fucked Cece on Valentine's Day when it was so obvious he couldn't stand her. Or how he ended up so buddy-buddy with the cop that led her arrest. The part that baffles me is that he's acting like I should be appreciative when really all I feel is gross. I never asked him to do those things. I just wanted him to make sure Kathryn had a fair shot.

"I'm glad it was taken care of." *Seriously, what else can I say right now?*

Jax stalks toward me, gaining on me even as I try to take two steps back for each one he takes forward. There's a predatory look in his eyes that makes me nervous—and makes me wish I never let go of the doorframe. He stalks me across the room until the backs of my knees hit the bed, my stomach sinking as I realize this was exactly what he wanted.

"What do you want?" I snap at him, trying to sound more confident than I feel.

"I did all that shit for *you*." His voice sounds slightly strangled. "So what do I want?" He hesitates, and for a second I think we're finally getting some-where. That he might find it in himself to be sincere for once, instead of being such an ass. Instead, he growls out, "What I want is to know how you're planning to thank me."

"Dammit, Jax." I shove him back, and to my surprise he lets me. "What's wrong with you?"

"You tell me," he shoots back, scowling like I'm the one in the wrong here.

I don't get him. It's not even like he's hot and cold with me—unless you count the heat of him coming onto me and the coldness of him being an ass about it. This would actually be a little easier if he was ever just freaking nice like a normal person. He's really fucked up, but when I think of the man downstairs, am I really that surprised? It's not like Ed Woods is a beacon of warmth and love.

These last few weeks have been too much, and now this just feels like a breaking point. I'm tired of playing this weird game with him. But I haven't forgotten the first day of school, and the way I won at the game of chicken he created. Jax Woods does not like to be caught off guard.

Which is why I throw myself at him, latching my arms around his neck as I kiss the ever loving hell out of him. He doesn't even kiss me back at first, but I lick the seam of his mouth to encourage him to open for me, and after that all hell breaks loose. He takes over control, his tongue pushes mine exactly where he wants it as his hands cup my ass, pulling me harder against him. Just as I start to feel myself losing complete control, I remember what I was doing in the first place.

He lets me go when I push against his chest, his eyes hooded as he blows out a long breath and watches me carefully. I grab the hem of my tank top and pull it over my head, reveling in the way uncertainty passes over his face.

When I unbutton my pants and start pushing those down my legs, he lunges for me. I'm half-afraid this plan is about to go horribly wrong, until I feel him yank my shorts back up my legs. "Dammit, Juliet."

"What? Isn't this what you wanted?" I taunt him, twisting so he can't quite get my shorts all the way back up. He's leaned down a little reaching for my shorts, so I arch my back to thrust my chest right into his face.

He hesitates, and for a second I can see his weakening resolve. Shit, I can even feel my own resolve weakening. If he doesn't put a stop to this, I'm not sure I'll be able to, either.

But he does, stepping back, completely out of reach as he looks at something just past my head instead of looking at my nearly exposed body. Funny how he's the one that dragged me here and now he's acting like an innocent schoolboy. Funny how easily the tables are turned when he realizes I'm better at this game of chicken then he is.

I'm starting to realize that despite what an asshole Jax is—and he definitely *is*—he's not nearly as much of a brute as he wants me to think. That last time, he really wanted me to think he would force himself on me without a second thought. This time, I see that's not at all true.

"I said," I continue to taunt him, "isn't this what you wanted? C'mon, Jax. Here I am. Do your worst." I hold my arms out, offering myself up to him on a silver platter. It doesn't get any easier than this, but he still doesn't look at me. "What, now you don't want to fuck me? Performance anxiety?"

He can't ignore that one, eyes cutting over to me with sheer disgust. "I'll fuck you when you beg me to, and not a goddamn second sooner. You *are* going to beg me, Juliet." He turns and is gone before I get a chance to respond. It's probably for the best. I wanted to tell him *fat chance of that*, but only one of us can be right, and I'm starting to worry that it might actually be him.

By the time I've collected myself and made it back downstairs, Jax is nowhere to be found. Governor Woods' security team is still standing guard though, so I hover nearby, hoping that he'll finish up soon.

A few minutes later, I get my wish. The security goons step to the side to let Governor Woods pass, the sitting-room door slamming open against the wall as he yanks it with far too much force. Whatever happened in there, he obviously isn't pleased.

He storms right past me, not bothering to acknowledge my presence at all. My first real thought is that I only hope he hasn't upset Pearl, especially when she's only lucid about two-thirds of the time. I don't want her to waste that precious time on an asshole like this.

"Have a nice day," I call out sarcastically to his back.

He freezes halfway to the door, turning back to me with a stone-faced expression. My face heats as he says just one thing: "Your lip gloss is smeared."

4

It's hard to believe the summer is already half over. I'm bent over, seeking out something new to read from the shelves in Hollis' office when a whistle startles me. I turn to see Ace taking up the whole doorway, watching me with his shoulder butting up against the frame. To the casual observer, he would look easygoing standing there like that, but I don't miss the way his muscles are bunched below the surface. He's worked up, even if he's not showing it. It's nice to know he's not immune to my charms— and by charms, I obviously mean my ass.

"What are you doing here?" I ask as I walk towards him and he meets me in the middle of the room. I wrap my arms around him and breathe him in. It's been too long since I've seen any of my guys. I haven't wanted to steal their summers away from them, even though every single one of them has bitched at me for seeing it that way.

"Your aunt made the nurse call and threaten my life if I didn't come get you out of the house," he answers with zero humor in his voice. I know Pearl well enough to know he's not joking. Plus, the nurse on duty right now is this tiny little thing that's absolutely terrified of Pearl and does everything she asks without question—even if it's threatening a teenage boy with murder.

I raise my eyebrows, surprised that Ace was the first call more than anything else. He shakes his head sheepishly, reading my mind. "The other guys are all out of town. I'm pretty sure she actually tried to call Jax first, but lucky for you this is Ed Woods' Hamptons week. It's the only vacation he actually takes with the family all year, mostly just so they can get Fourth of July photos for his website."

"Well, I'm glad it's you." I pull at him until he lowers his head to me, offering me his lips but letting me take the lead.

It's the first real kiss I've gotten to share with him. There's nothing behind it. No alcohol, no emotional vulnerability, nothing. This kiss is one just for us. For no reason other than wanting to kiss each other because we care for each other.

His mouth parts for me almost immediately as I keep trying to inch closer. As I kiss him, my squirming must get to him, because he pulls back and lets out a groan. Before I know what's happening, he's pushing me up against a row of bookshelves, his hands lifting me by the ass as he pulls me up to a more comfortable height. I wrap my legs around him, marveling at how easily he holds me up.

Ace blinks at me, looking shocked himself about how we ended up here. If I weren't so damn hot right now, I might laugh. Instead, I whimper. I don't mean to, it just slips out. This guy is hot as hell in the best kind of way because it's like he has no idea how goddamn sexy he is.

He's so open and vulnerable, but also just so damn masculine in the way he carries himself. Partially because of his size. A guy this big could never be mistaken for anything but masculine honestly. Not to mention the other decidedly masculine thing about him, which I just so happen to be rubbing up against like I'm in heat or something. *But it feels so fucking good.*

Ace's mouth descends on mine, not giving me a chance to second guess how forward I'm being with him. He must like it, a little voice says in the back of my head, otherwise why would he pin you up against the wall like this? *No, not just the wall, the bookshelves.*

This is like the ultimate wet dream right here.

Until he pulls away and groans out, "We should stop."

What? No! Fuck me against the bookshelves, right fucking now! I think it, but I don't say it out loud. I nod my head as he backs up so he can let me down. I don't make it easy for him, forcing him to let me slide straight down his body and getting an excellent feel of his body in the process. Can't blame a girl for wanting to feel the goods—not when the goods are this *good*.

"Sorry, I just—"

"It's okay, you don't have to explain. Stop means stop, Ace. For any reason." And even though Jax and I apparently aren't living by that same rule, I'm not about to pressure Ace into anything. There's still a sore spot in my chest whenever I think about what Celia Harrington did to him. She never should have put her hands on him, and I think that makes me pay ten times more attention to making sure I'm not putting him in an uncomfortable position.

Thinking about Celia makes my eyes automatically move to his arm. There's still a small scar where Celia stabbed him over Spring Break. He catches me looking and rubs a finger along the ridged edge.

"I don't want this to plague us forever," he tells me, making me feel bad for drawing attention back to this topic. "What happened with Celia was fucked up, but it has nothing to do with us. I want you. Trust me." He blows out a long breath. "But right now, I've gotta get you outta here before Pearl makes good on her promise to have a hitman take me out. If anyone has actual hitmen running around somewhere, my money's definitely on Pearl Lexington." He shudders.

"Fine." I pout. "Where are you taking me, then?"

"Home," he answers with a grin.

One of my eyebrows goes up as his grin morphs into a secretive little smile. "Your home?"

He nods, but doesn't offer anything more than that. Still, I can feel excitement bubbling up when I remember what Patrick told me about Ace's house. A horse farm. There definitely aren't horse farms in Nikon Park.

"Well, what are you waiting for? Let's go!" I give him a shove, thinking I might push him towards the door. I'm hilarious. Ace doesn't budge an inch.

"Did you really think that would work?" he teases.

This guy... he's really something else. All the heaviness of these past weeks seems to melt away as he takes me home with him for the first time. There's just something about Ace that makes being with him easy. I'm glad he's the one I'm spending this time away with for a little while. That feeling amplifies tenfold when we pull through the gates to his family's property.

My eyes are practically glued to the window as we drive down a long, winding driveway, passing fields dotted with horses. There's a big barn out to the side, Ace stops there instead of pulling all the way around to the house. He barely has the car in park before I'm jumping out, my wide eyes trying to take everything in at once.

"If I'd known this was the way to your heart, I

would have brought you here a long time ago." Ace grins as he comes around the car to take my hand. "Let me show you the babies."

Baby animals. Damn. Ace really knows the way to a girl's heart.

We walk hand-in-hand into the barn, my eyes going impossibly wider as I realize this wasn't at all what I was expecting. This place has to be state-of-the art. I might not know much about horses or farms, but even I can see that this place is big money. Especially since on top of the facilities being stunning, there are at least a dozen people meandering about, doing work that I don't exactly understand but that looks important.

Ace walks me down the center aisle of the barn, smiling patiently at me when I stop to gawk over a gigantic horse thrusting its head out of its stall towards me. "Here." He reaches into his pocket and hands me a wrapped peppermint candy.

I raise an eyebrow.

"For the horse," he explains. "You can feed him."

"Really? He eats candy?"

Ace grins down at me as he nods, and the sight of it makes butterflies break out in my stomach. This is so nice.

I unwrap the peppermint and start to hand it to the horse before I think better of it. Growing up, one of my friends had a goat in her neighbor's backyard that we used to feed half our snacks to. We learned real quick to put our hands flat or risk losing our fingers. I flatten my hand, the corners of my lips curling up when I see the approval in Ace's eyes.

The big horse nips gently at my hand to take the peppermint. His little whiskers on his nose tickle my hand, making me giggle. For a second, I'm lost in the moment. I love animals, but I never had the chance to be around them a lot growing up. We certainly never had money for pets—my fake parents barely had money to feed ourselves sometimes. Every once in a while I'd spend a few days sneaking scraps to a stray cat, but they never hung around for long.

The memory kills my butterflies.

I've spent so much time saying goodbye to things, and I can't help thinking that the biggest goodbye of all is breathing down my neck. Every day, Pearl gets a little less lucid. A year ago, I didn't even know she existed, but now the idea of losing her breaks something in me. She's the only real connection I have to the person I was supposed to be. When she's gone, I'll be the only Lexington left.

"Hey." Ace grabs my hand again so he can turn me towards him. "It's okay," he says as he wraps me up in his arms. I'm not nearly as good at hiding my feelings as I wish I was. I sniffle, trying to hold back the tears threatening to fall.

A sudden, very firm nudge pushes my head to the side. A laugh escapes me as I turn to see the horse I just fed trying to get my attention again. He nudges me again, lower this time so that he basically head-butts my chest.

"A guy who knows what he likes," Ace teases as he takes out another peppermint and hands it to me. I feed it to my new buddy, but then my eyes slide over to the horse in the next stall who's now shoving its head out to eye us.

"That horse wants a peppermint, too," I point out with a pout. Ace eyes me, and I'm fully prepared for him to tell me I'm being silly. It would take forever to feed every horse in here, even with half of the stalls empty—I'm assuming because they belong to the horses that are outside. I wipe my hands together, not wanting to make a big deal out of it even though I really do feel a little bad that the other horses are missing out.

I'm not looking when Ace says my name. "Juliet," he repeats, and this time I look up. Just in time for him to hold out two fistfuls of wrapped candies for me. I gape at him as I take a handful from him. I can't hold nearly as much as he can at one time but that doesn't seem to bother him.

"Really?" I can't imagine this is that fun for him, watching me feed treats to his horses.

He holds his hands out to the side so they're out of the way as he leans in and kisses me long and slow on the lips. When he pulls away, he shakes his head, but he's still grinning. "You've got a big heart. I can promise you one thing, J, I'm never gonna stifle that.

There's nothing wrong with having a lot of love to share."

As we stare intently at one another, I know with absolute certainty that he's not just talking about feeding the horses. He's reassuring me about our arrangement in the most roundabout possible way. Ace is really good at talking to me about things, but one thing I have noticed is he's not so good at the talking when it's about him. This is his way of being clear about his feelings. It's the first time he's really said anything in that regards since Pearl first got back to Lexington Estate, so it's nice to have the confirmation again.

I lean in to kiss him again. "Let's feed some damn horses, then!"

We spend the whole next hour in the barn, Ace following me around with a content smile as I feed horses until my hands are covered in layers of spit thicker than my skin. With a laugh, Ace leads me to a bathroom in the barn that's even nicer than the ones at Lexington Estate. I know horses cost a lot of money, but I had no idea Ace's family was quite this well-off. He's pretty unassuming, honestly. If I ran into him as a stranger on the street I'd never guess this is the kind of place he lives.

"You ready to go?" Ace asks when I step out of the bathroom, a glint in his eye that lets me know he's joking.

I fake a shocked gasp. "I was promised baby animals."

"Honestly, I started to think you'd forgotten while you were busy making friends in here." His smile only gets wider. I think he's enjoying how much I'm loving this. It makes sense. This is his natural habitat, and now I've stepped right in and embraced it.

"Have you brought other girls here?" I blurt out. I don't know why I'm suddenly so put off by the idea. It's not like I expected to be the first person he ever cared about—I just don't like the idea that he shared this with someone else. That he smiled that same smile at some other girl's enthusiasm.

Based on the way he grimaces, I don't think I need to be so worried. "I brought Margo Yorke here once in the ninth grade." The name sounds familiar, but I can't picture who he's talking about. "I thought things were getting serious."

I can tell there's a *but* coming, so when he falls silent I prompt him, "But…?"

"But, uh, it turned out she'd only been hanging around because she had a crush on Sadie. The whole time I thought Margo and I were dating, she thought I was just a really bad wingman." His cheeks tinge pink as he ducks his head, clearly embarrassed. Poor Ace, he really can't seem to catch a break, can he? Which is crazy, because he's such a goddamn dreamboat.

"Well, just to be sure there's no confusion, you and I are definitely dating." I wrap a finger around one of his belt-loops and tug until he indulges me by stepping closer. When he does, I take a step back, then another and another.

Ace smirks as I end up leading us around a quiet corner where bales of hay are stacked high, obscuring the view for anyone who happens to pass by. I offer him a coy smile, opening my mouth to ask if this is okay, but the words are stolen right out of my mouth as he grabs my hips and swings me around so that my back is to the wooden wall.

I run frenzied hands over the muscles of his back and shoulders as his hands slide down to my ass and scoop me up just like he did in the library. I smile against his mouth as his hard body presses into mine. I'm not sure how we keep ending up in this position but *damn do I like it.*

As we kiss, Ace keeps one hand holding me up, but the other slips under the edge of my t-shirt, grazing the bare skin just above the waistband of my shorts. I shiver as he gently runs his finger along the line of my waistband. He doesn't go any further than that, but damn if it isn't some of the best foreplay I've ever had. Probably even more so because it's so natural, neither of us rushing to turn it into anything more.

The sound of footsteps followed by hooves passing right by finally makes us break apart. We're both panting as we grin at each other, both having thoroughly enjoyed ourselves. It shows, too. Ace's hair is all kinds of fucked up from where I was running my hands through it, and I can't imagine mine looks much better. With a light laugh, I let my head fall to rest against his shoulder.

"Juliet?"

"Hmm?"

He laughs. "We still haven't made it to see the babies."

5

After my day at Ace's family's farm, the floodgates seem to open and Pearl puts on twice the pressure for me to get out of the house. *"You're driving me crazy, girl. Go bother someone else for a while."* I don't think she means to be an asshole about it, my hovering is just driving her crazy. Though, after spending half the summer cooped up by Pearl's bedside, I have to admit it feels nice to be getting out of the house again.

I don't do anything that special. I spend some time with the guys just hanging out. Patrick drives me up to Churchill Point a few times. Ace takes me to get ice cream and doesn't even make fun of me for getting twice as many toppings as I did the first time.

Now, Smith is home from the cruise he had to go on with his mom since Sadie is still at Banner-Hill and couldn't go on their girls' trip after all. So that's where he's taking me today, Banner-Hill to visit Sadie.

We spend the drive playing roulette with the radio, pressing the buttons quickly several times in a row and then letting it stop on a random channel. The rule is that we have to finish listening to any song we land on, which ends in a lot of laughter when we somehow end up landing mostly on kid-friendly stations and some old school church music. We even happen upon one station that's hosting Christmas in July.

Several times, I catch Smith staring over at me as we roll down stretches of highway. "What?" I finally ask and he just shakes his head, smiling like he's got some secret he doesn't want to share.

"Tell me," I plead, reaching over to jab my finger in his ribs. He winces even as he laughs.

"I was just remembering how you were so distracted by how hot I was that you broke your phone the first time we met." He sounds so casual about it as my mouth falls open. I poke him again, harder this time.

"You asshole! I dropped my phone because you startled me."

"That's not how I remember it." He's straight-faced as he says it, but I can see now the smile he's trying to hold back. He's so fucking cute, even when he's being a teasing asshole.

Still, "You're conveniently forgetting the part where you grabbed me so hard I had bruises for the next three days." There's no way in hell I'm ready to just gloss over what an asshole he was at first. He's redeemed himself by now I feel like, sure, but it's much better to forgive than to forget.

"Shit." He looks over at my waist as if the marks would somehow still be there, but I'm wearing a crop top today and there's definitely nothing marring my skin now. Luckily for me, the only grabbing anyone has been doing of me lately is the hot kind, not the asshole kind. "Thanks for reminding me," he grumbles.

"You're the one that did it," I point out with a shrug. He's not gonna make me feel bad for bringing it up, not when he's the one that started those issues when we first met—not me.

I would have been perfectly happy to have shown up here and had it be easy sailing. I think about that sometimes, how different things might have gone if the guys hadn't made it so hard for me when I first got here. I like to think things would have been the same, that I would have been drawn to the same people, but I'm not sure how much truth there is to that. The way they treated me, it wasn't right, but it toughened me up in a way that I needed to be able to survive this long in Patience.

The only one I still haven't forgiven is Jax. Not that he cares. He hasn't been back around since the bedroom incident—which is definitely for the best.

"You know I'm sorry for that crap right?" Smith growls, interrupting the train of thought I definitely don't need to be following down the rabbit hole right now.

I nod. Yes, of course I know he's sorry.

"Good." He nods, too. "I'd prefer not to end up in the doghouse alongside Jax."

What the hell is that supposed to mean exactly? I don't get a chance to ask before Smith is telling me we're here.

For some reason, when I pictured visiting Sadie in rehab, I pictured it like a movie scene of a jail visit. We'd pull up to an electric fence surrounding an imposing concrete building and we'd go inside and sit on opposite sides of the glass as we talked to Sadie through a telephone. That was so dumb of me.

In reality, we pull up to Banner-Hill and for a minute I think we made a wrong turn and ended up at someone's mega-mansion by mistake. The only reason I figure out that's not what happened is because Smith gets out of the car and comes around to open my door, making it clear that this is exactly where we were supposed to be. I'm surprised there's not at least a sign out here or something.

Inside, a serene looking woman at the front desk greets us and escorts us to a back patio overlooking an Olympic size pool. This place is seriously ridiculous—and not at all the prison I imagined.

We sit at a table outside to wait for Sadie, Smith turning to me as soon as the woman that showed us out here leaves us to ourselves. He offers me his hand, which I take without hesitation. I'm not sure why he suddenly looks so uncomfortable until he opens his mouth.

"I'm sorry about that back there in the car. I didn't mean to bring up all that shit and I do obviously know it was my fault your phone got broken. I mean, it was a crappy phone, but still it was yours and I shouldn't have startled you like that."

"I'd love to say it's okay because you replaced it, but…" *But you replaced it with a phone you manipulated so that I couldn't talk to my best friend.*

"Have you talked to that guy?" Smith looks away, looking out over the empty pool instead of meeting my eyes. *That guy.* He doesn't even want to say Jake's name. Hell, after what I learned over Spring Break, I'm still not sure if I do either. I thought I could trust Jake. Even with things so bad between us and us not talking, I never in a million years thought he would ever tell my fake mom anything. Lynne Brown treated me like hell long before I found out the truth and went home to Patience, and Jake knows that. The fact that he told her I was living in a nice house —and the fact that I'm pretty damn sure he's how she got my number—I just mostly try not to think about it anymore.

So, when I answer Smith's question, all I say is a hard, "Nope."

I'm relieved when he doesn't say anything. Smith hasn't made it any secret that he doesn't think much of Jake. It's ironic really, how the one guy he's jealous of is the one guy who's not actually around.

"Jules!" The squeal of my name puts an effective end to our sudden awkward silence.

I jump out of my seat even before I see her. "Oh my god, you look so good," I tell her as she throws her arms around me. I'm not just saying it to be nice, she really looks fantastic. I pull back to take another good look at her. Her hair is back to its normal blonde, though still cut shorter than when we first met. She's wearing light makeup but a fierce looking wrap dress that sparkles in the sunlight as she steps over to hug Smith next.

"Love you, brother. Glad you're here. Now go find something to entertain yourself." Sadie shoves Smith twice across the patio until he's back at the doors that lead inside.

"What!" He tries to plant his feet but nearly loses his balance thanks to her continued shoving.

She rolls her eyes at him. "You visit me all the time. I want to hangout with Juliet without you. Don't worry, I'll only tell her *some* of your most embarrassing childhood stories while you're gone. Now go."

"At least let me stay out here and go take a walk or something," he protests with a huff.

She stops pushing him, lighting up like she hadn't even considered that as an option. "Nevermind, you can stay here. We're going for a walk." She waves me towards the two glass steps leading from the patio out into the yard—which looks like it goes on forever with no other buildings in sight.

Smith groans. "I can't believe I drove all this way just to sit here by myself. Good thing I charged my phone," he grumbles.

We barely make it half the length of the pool before she pauses and throws her arms around me again. "God, it's so good to see you." When she pulls back, she adds, "I was worried you would change your mind and not want to come."

"What? Why?"

"I was so horrible to you before I came back here... I wasn't in my right mind at all." She opens her mouth like she's going to go on but I slap a hand over her mouth without thinking about it. Her eyes widen in surprise.

"Sorry." I blow out a frustrated breath. "Apparently today is the day for re-opening old wounds." I laugh nervously. "But Sadie, I don't need any more apologies from you. I get it. You were grieving and you needed someone to blame at the time, I know it wasn't personal." I wish it had been someone besides me, obviously, but I can't change the past now and neither can she. I'm ready to move forward, and I'm hoping she is too. I can't imagine she'll be staying at this place much longer. Smith said she would definitely be home before school started again, and that date keeps inching closer and closer.

"You're too forgiving. With most of us, anyway. I hear you're still making Jax sweat it out." She smirks as I throw my head back with a groan.

"Seriously? Why does everyone keep bringing up

Jax? I seriously can't hang out with anyone anymore without him coming up at least once." I'm so tired of talking about Jax. I'm not sure why everyone is so worried about me blowing him off. It's not like he's done anything to deserve more than that from me. In fact, I personally think I've been far friendlier towards him than he deserves just by acknowledging that he exists. Screw Jax Woods. I don't owe him anything.

Sadie starts walking again and I follow suit. "Touchy subject, I guess," she says casually, shrugging it off.

"For obvious reasons." Or has everyone else forgotten all the shit he's done to me? I swore there would be consequences for Jax Woods, and now there are. I'm not melting into a puddle at his feet. I'm starting to think that's a far better punishment than I could have imagined, based on how often other people keep bringing it up. I can't imagine they'd be doing that if Jax wasn't bothered in some way by it.

"Tell me what else is going on. Smith is no good at gossip, he never knows what's important and what's not." That would explain why she's concerned about Jax. He's the one person Smith pays extra close attention to—besides me, at least.

"I don't know much," I admit. "I've been sort of out of the loop with everything going on with Pearl."

Sadie's expression softens. We got to talk over the

phone after I took Pearl home, and I told her everything Pearl and the doctors had told me about her health. There are still more questions than answers, with her tumor growing inconsistently. Every time the doctors check her, they seem confused, which I don't think really bodes well for us. Pearl and I have an agreement not to talk about time anymore. Mostly because I got tired of her acting like it would be any day now, and she got tired of me going along like we had years left to go. The only happy medium we could find was just agreeing not to talk about it anymore at all.

"Knowing that woman, she'll go when she's ready and not a damn minute before." *Now there's something we can both agree on.*

We fall into silence for a few minutes as we draw closer to the tree line that I assume marks the end of the property. Or at least as far as I imagine Sadie's allowed to go. It looks pretty creepy back in those dark woods, a sharp contrast to the pretty glass building behind us.

"There was an orgy back there last week," Sadie announces out of nowhere, pointing right in the direction that I was looking. There's nothing through the trees but pitch darkness, but I guess that's about all you need for an orgy. *Rehab orgy... there has to be rules against that or something.* Sadie continues, "Okay, no one's actually confirmed it, but that's what the rumor mill is saying. In fact—" She stops and looks behind us like she's checking to

57

make sure no one snuck up on us out here. "People are saying Killian Lake was involved."

I nearly choke on my own saliva. "Killian Lake is here?" My head twists to either side as if I'm expecting him to materialize out of nowhere. Sadie laughs, clearly enjoying my reaction.

"Down, girl, I think you've got enough boys to juggle without adding a guy like that to the mix." She's not wrong, but *Killian Lake*.

The guy's a total heartthrob. Not to mention the leading man of most of my late night fantasies—and probably those of every other teenage girl in existence. He's a musician, one of those hot singer-songwriter types that's been tearing up the music charts. I had no idea he was in rehab. I would have expected that to be all over the gossip rags and entertainment sites. Killian Lake is a big deal. The kind of guy who you call by his full name every damn time you talk about him. *Killian Lake*. God, I'm practically panting just thinking of him.

"I'm not really supposed to tell anyone about him being here. So, keep it to yourself, okay? We all had to sign special NDAs when he showed up." I guess that explains why it's not a front-page story on every gossip blog in the country right now.

"I won't say anything." I have a weird thought. "Wait, you weren't in the orgy, were you?" Because that would be some seriously red flag behavior I think.

She laughs so loud she startles some birds out of

the trees. "God, don't I wish? If Killian Lake invited me to an orgy, I would go, Juliet. No questions asked." *Me too, probably. Sheesh, it is Killian-fucking-Lake we're talking about.*

"Yeah," I concede, "that's fair actually."

"Right? It's much less of a stretch for you though, I guess." She snorts lightly. Her words are light and teasing, but they make me stop short just as we were starting to walk again. Her words might be light-hearted, but there's something else. A sort of judgement layered underneath as if I wouldn't notice it.

For a second, we look at each other both with passive faces, but then Sadie is the first to break. She looks the opposite way, squinting when the sun shines right in her face. "I'm sorry," she apologizes, sounding much more authentic than she did just now. "I shouldn't be like that. Love is love, right? It's not really my business. I just... don't want to see my brother get hurt," she admits.

"And I don't want to hurt your brother." I'm not sure why she would think otherwise.

"He's in love with you, you know." My heart freezes up in my chest, forgetting to beat as I absorb those words. "I'm sure he hasn't said it yet, especially not with the whole Jax thing still on the back of his mind. But I guess I'm just a little worried that he'll let his feelings make him blind. That he'd agree to anything you wanted just to keep you, even if it was hurting him."

For someone that just apologized for being a bit

of an asshole before, she's sure throwing a hell of a lot of knives with her words now. In just a few sentences, she's managed to cut right to my biggest insecurity: that I'm being unfair by keeping all three of my boys. But fuck, every time I picture trying to cut them loose—any of them—I find myself struggling to breathe. If they were really bothered by our arrangement, would they say something? I think back to Patrick at prom. He wasn't thrilled, but he stayed. But didn't he only do that because he thought he'd lose me otherwise? Dammit, why does this have to be so hard? And why did Sadie have to bring this up now?

"Look, it's none of my business, okay? Smith would be really mad if he knew I'd said anything." She glances back nervously to where he's sitting on the patio, facing out towards us as if he's watching us walk the grounds. Seems to me like Sadie's saying a lot of things she shouldn't today.

"Sadie." I wait until she looks at me, wanting to make sure I have her full attention before I say my piece. "I showed a lot of grace when you came to me in the spring to try to make amends. It would have been easy to turn my back, to say you hurt me and I wouldn't give you the chance to do it again. Since that's not what I did, I want you to consider this our line in the sand moment." Her face falls, but I don't even feel a little bad about it. Our friendship needs this if it's ever going to survive. "When you get back from rehab, you can either accept how things are or find a new pity-bestie, because I'm done playing that role and I'm not interested in your judgments."

"I don't—"

I shake my head and cut her off. "If you'll excuse me, I think it's time I go home." I take a few steps away from her before I can't resist turning back. "Not that it's any of your business, but I'm in love with your brother. So, finish getting your shit together, Sadie. Then maybe you'll finally get to see that for yourself."

She stands in stunned silence as I turn on my heel and stalk the rest of the way across the yard, back to Smith, who doesn't even question me when I tell him I'll be waiting in the car when he's ready to go. It wasn't my brightest moment, blurting out that I was in love with Smith for the first time to his sister instead of saying it to him. He deserves to know, even though I haven't worked up the nerve to say it properly since that day I accidentally let the words slip in the hallway.

Maybe Sadie will tell him. Hell, so what if she does? I love Smith, and I'm not going to let someone take that away from me just because they think love has to be black and white. I lean my head back against the seat of the car and remember Ace's words.

There's nothing wrong with having a lot of love to share.

6

Pearl isn't doing well. It's the very end of the summer, only days away from the back-to-school bash Allie Townsend is throwing, and the only thing I can focus on is how delirious Pearl has suddenly gotten. The doctors all say it's a normal progression of her diagnosis, but there's nothing reassuring about that. I don't want normal progression. I want a goddamn miracle.

I'm surprised none of the guys have shown up unannounced yet, though I'm sure it's coming soon. I've stopped answering my phone, too afraid that I might get tied up in a call and miss Pearl needing something. I barely even drag myself away to go to the bathroom or shower anymore unless the nurses swear not to leave her side for even a second.

No one ever prepared me for this. I've never watched anyone I love die before.

"You always carry such a heavy heart," Pearl's

sleepy voice carries to me. I was curled up in a chair reading, but I drop my book the second she speaks so that I can lean closer. The last few days, she starts to trail off in the middle of sentences. I've learned that if I get close, I can sometimes catch the tail end of things before she's falling asleep again.

"I'm not sure what that means," I tell her, watching the way her eyes struggle to stay open. She's deteriorating much faster now than before, just like she said she would.

"It means you need to lighten up, girl." She cackles at her own little joke, and I can't help but laugh, too. It's ironic really, this woman who was desperate for me to learn the ropes of high society, now telling *me* to lighten up.

Resting my arms on the edge of her bed, I tell her, "I'll lighten up when life stops being so hard."

"What's so damn hard about it?" *Jesus, it's so jarring to hear her curse.* She's only done it a handful of times in the last week, and each time actually seems worse than the last. "You're a beautiful—and very rich—girl with four hot boyfriends. Sounds like a breeze to me."

"Three," I correct her with a smile.

She shoots me a look much like the ones she shot me when I first came. The kind she used to tell me I wasn't doing something to her liking. "I'm still counting the Woods boy, whether you like it or not."

No matter how out of it she gets, these are the details she remembers. She never forgets that I'm

63

dating more than one boy, and she never forgets to remind me that she still counts Jax as one of them. She barely remembers my name some days, but of course *this* she can't seem to let go of. And I indulge her every damn time because I want to appreciate all the little moments like this that we have left. This is by far the most time we've spent together, and even though she won't be around to remember it, I know I always will.

"It's such a shame I've ruined your summer, dear."

I blink as warm tears start to fall. I'm really glad the nurse is on a lunch break and not here to see this. My voice is thick with emotion as I tell her, "You didn't ruin anything. This is the best summer I've ever had."

It's the truth, too. A summer spent with family, even if it's just me and Pearl and the circumstances aren't ideal. This is the kind of thing I always dreamed of, just with a few extra details I absolutely never could have imagined. Plus, I've gotten a few stolen moments with my boys, and those have been just as precious as this time I've gotten to spend with Pearl. I wouldn't change this summer even if given the chance—unless it was to make it so Pearl was never sick in the first place.

"Next summer..." She starts to falter and my lips curl down. I hate when she trails off in the middle of a sentence. It always leaves me wondering what she meant to say. And it always makes me panic that they'll be her last words.

Her eyes pop open again. "Next summer take those nice boys of yours to the beach house. They can skip the fancy vacations for one year. Spend some real, quality time together. Learn each other's secrets." She yawns, and I can tell she's struggling to stay awake.

This has been one of her more lucid moments, and my heart-rate drops as I realize this might be one of the few chances I have left to ask her that one burning question I haven't been able to forget.

I clear my throat twice before I can get the words out. "Pearl, I need to ask you something about Hollis." *Oh my god, am I really going to do this?* I don't have a choice. It's now or never. I'm not sure I could live with myself if I don't at least try to get answers.

"Oh, Hollis." She tsks. "What about him, dear?"

"Did Hollis hire the Browns to kill my mother?" Time seems to move in slow-motion as Pearl turns her head to look directly at me, more clarity in her eyes than I've seen in weeks. There's a solemnness to them, too, and I think I know what the answer is going to be even before she says it.

"Oh, Juliet. You're going to find out eventually, anyway, aren't you?" She moves her fingers around strangely, and it takes me a second before I realize she's trying to reach for my hand. I curl my fingers gently around hers. "All he ever wanted was to bring you home—and instead he did the exact opposite."

I raise my eyes to stare at the wall, blinking slowly as I try to process her words. I want her answer to be different. I want her to be chastising me for saying something so outrageous. For casting a bad light over Hollis' legacy. Instead, it sounds like she's confirming what Lynne said. Could my own grandfather really have hired the junkies that killed my parents? It sounds like something out of a bad TV show.

"He wanted my mother dead?" I whisper the question. I'd been so excited just to have a family legacy that I don't know if I stopped enough to consider what that legacy might be. This? This is not the legacy I want. A family ripped apart from the inside.

"Courtney Bernard was a monster." Pearl sounds so cavalier about it.

Courtney Bernard. I guess I shouldn't be surprised to hear Pearl use my mother's maiden name. It's clear Hollis and Pearl never considered her a Lexington. What could have been so wrong with her to make them dislike her so much? Being new money instead of old money—and liking modern touches—didn't make a person a monster.

As if reading my mind, Pearl lets go of my hand. "Get the photo album, dear." I'm not sure which she means until she adds, "The wedding album on the bottom shelf." She gestures to the built-ins by the fireplace.

I stand up and go where she pointed, fingering the books along the bottom shelf until I come to the one I realize is a wedding album. I haven't seen it before, probably because it was hidden down here among the dust and old copies of classic children's books. I blow across the cover, watching dust scatter into the air as the dirty gray cover becomes something more like an off-white. I imagine the book was actually pure white at some point, but time hasn't been kind to it.

"Turn to the third page," Pearl tells me when I start to hand her the album. She closes her eyes as if she can't bear to look with me. I flip three pages in just like she asked.

I recognize my parents from other pictures of them, the two of them standing at the altar on their wedding day. There's something weird about this picture of them. They don't look happy the way you expect people to on their wedding day.

"Look at the front row," Pearl continues. "Do you see the man in the pinstripe suit?" It takes me a minute to see who she's talking about—mostly because it's hard to tear my eyes away from my parents. "That man was Benny Tribeca."

My head snaps up so I can gawk at her. "The mobster?"

She nods. Benny Tribeca isn't a name anyone around here could forget. He made national news a few years ago when the feds finally brought him in. He was running an illegal adoption ring, which was just a nicer way of describing human trafficking. He had babies kidnapped from all over the world to sell to desperate parents who couldn't get approved by the real adoption agencies. Everyone was talking about it for months. The guy was as scummy as they come.

"Why was he at their wedding?" Already, I can tell I'm not going to like where this story is heading.

"Courtney had quite the affinity for trouble. It didn't matter that your father would have spent every red cent he had to please her, she wanted trouble and went asking for it. But you don't get into bed with a man like Benny without consequences." Fucking hell, I hope she only means getting into bed in the figurative sense. "He showed up to the wedding to threaten her. She didn't just owe him power, she owed him introductions. Now that she was a Lexington in name, he wanted those connections. Hollis had friends in high places."

Her eyes start to drift again. "Pearl!" She startles at her name and I mutter an apology, but I have to hear everything once and for all. "Tell me the rest. What happened with Benny?"

Her head nods a few times as she struggles to remember where we were. "Yes, well, she put him off, that Benny. He didn't like that much. She didn't want her fancy friends knowing she'd been fooling around with a mobster." *Okay, not just figurative maybe.* My heart is beating painfully in my chest as a sudden fear strikes me. Is Pearl about to tell me Benny Tribeca is my real father? She might give me a goddamn stroke. "And then you came along." *Here it goes.* "Your father's pride and joy. Hollis' pride and joy. The most beautiful baby anyone had ever seen. And all Courtney saw was a chance to get Benny off her back."

"What?" My voice is small.

"People would have paid good money for a blue-blooded little girl like you." Pearl makes a little growly noise in her throat. It would be funny, if the words she was saying weren't so fucking heartbreaking. I wasn't just raised by monsters—I was born to one too.

"What the fuck!" I drop the wedding book, not caring at all that it falls to the floor. Right now, I'd be happy to throw it into a fire and watch it burn. What the fuck was wrong with the woman that birthed me that she was willing to trade me off to a mobster? And for what? Just so her society friends didn't find out where she liked to get her thrills? I thought nothing could be worse than what the Browns did, but this? This is actually worse. So much worse.

"Your father came to Hollis for help when he realized what she'd done. They paid Benny off, sent him away, but they knew they'd never be able to trust Courtney after that. So, they made a decision to do what was needed to protect you." Pearl's eyes are drooping again, but this time I don't care. I think I've got the gist of things now—which is already far more than I ever wanted to know. "They weren't supposed to shoot until your father got you out of the crosshairs. Never should have trusted a pair of druggies to stick to the plan…"

With those last words, she drifts off back to sleep. It doesn't seem fair, how peaceful she looks seconds after rocking my whole world. I pace the length of the room until I start to worry I'm wearing the floor down.

Every time I think I'm starting to come to terms with the reality of who I am, someone goes and drops another bombshell. I've spent months terrified to find out Hollis was the villain in my life story, only to find out it was actually my mother this whole time. Hollis tried to save me. And my dad tried to protect me, giving up his own life in the process. This is all too much. I wait a few more minutes for the nurse to return, then excuse myself to go lay down.

In my room, I close the curtains up tight so the room is pitch black, and then curl up in the center of my bed. I think about reaching out to one of my boys, knowing any of them would be here to comfort me in a heartbeat. Then I decide against it. For the moment, what I think I really need is to grieve alone. I bury my face in my pillow and let everything pour out of me. The months of being unwelcome. The chaos of Kathryn's death and everything that came after. And now this, finally discovering the truth of what happened the night my name was stolen from me. The only comfort I have is knowing that no one will ever be able to steal the name Juliet Lexington from me again.

7

I force a smile on my face as yet another person whose name I don't know offers to get me a drink. I've told every single one of them *no*, worried that it's just a ruse someone made up to drug my drink and make a fool of me somehow. I grew up thinking I had trust issues, but that was nothing compared to how I feel now. After Pearl dropped that bomb about my mother, I catch myself looking over my shoulder even more now than before.

"Juliet!" I turn just in time for Allie Townsend to throw her arms around me. This is her back to school party, but I've never had an actual conversation with her—despite how much time she's spent at our lunch table drooling over the boys, particularly Jax.

"Uh, hi," I tell her, carefully twisting out of her grasp. She's clearly had too much to drink already.

"I'm so glad you came! I asked Smith if you would

be here, but he said he wasn't sure." She's looking at me with an intensity that makes me uncomfortable. I told Smith I wasn't sure if I was coming because I hadn't wanted to, but Pearl hadn't taken no for an answer. She doesn't seem to remember telling me about my mother, but she's been able to tell I'm moping around more than usual. Her words, not mine.

She told me if I didn't come to this party of my own free will then she was going to start making calls for everyone to come to our house instead. Obviously, that was the last thing either of us really wanted right now. So, here I am.

Allie loops her arm through mine and starts dragging me further into her house as I stare over at her, bewildered. "Has anyone offered you a drink yet? I can have someone get you one." She taps the person closest to her at the moment and starts to ask them to do it, but I interrupt.

"I'd really rather get my own drink, Allie." That way no one will bother me later about the fact that I'm definitely not here to get drunk. I'll fill a cup with water or juice or something and no one really has to be the wiser. Everyone's going to be too drunk soon to notice whether I'm drinking or not, anyway.

"Of course!" Allie points towards a room I'm assuming is the kitchen and then starts tugging me that way. I'm indescribably relieved when we reach the kitchen and she lets go of me. "I think someone's looking for you," she says half under her breath. "I'll come find you later." She vanishes before I can tell her that's not necessary. I'm not sure why she would think she needs to come find me again. We're not friends; I barely know her.

It's not until I take my eyes off her retreating form that I realize what she was talking about. Jax is staring at me from across the kitchen. I consider tucking tail and following Allie, but the second our eyes make contact Jax is headed my way.

There's no running from him now I guess. I steel myself for whatever is coming. We haven't seen or spoken to each other in weeks. Not since that whole debacle in my bedroom.

"Juliet," he says my name as he comes to a stop in front of me.

"Jax."

His eyes trail down, giving me a good once over, his gaze lingering on my bare legs under the skirt I'm wearing tonight. His tongue darts out to lick the corner of his mouth, and I catch myself staring at the motion. Clearing my throat, I force my eyes back to his and wait for him to do the same. His lips curl up into a smirk.

He doesn't say anything, he's still just staring at me. The room around us is so crowded and loud, but just standing here with him, all I can notice is the silence hanging between us.

"Are you ready to beg me?" My mind goes blank for a second before his words really register.

"I'm not begging you for shit," I tell him, crossing my arms over my chest as I frown up at him. *Fuck this guy, seriously.* I can't for the life of me understand why everyone's been defending him for weeks. He's still the same sleazy asshole that put my body on display for all of our classmates last year. Anyone insinuating he might have feelings for me has clearly lost their damn mind.

Jax's eyes darken as I start to turn to leave. "Don't walk away from me," he growls as he grabs my arm. I'm so over this game. I jerk my arm out of his grasp and level him with a dark look of my own.

"Put your hands on me like that again and I'm going to do a lot worse than walking away from you. I'm not scared of you because of who your daddy is, Woods."

He works his jaw. "If you didn't want me putting my hands on you, then you wouldn't have shown up here dressed like a slut. Don't act like you didn't wear that for my benefit."

I don't take even one second to think about it—I just fucking deck him as hard as I can, right in the jaw. He staggers back, clearly surprised by the blow even though I know he's had worse. I wince as my hand starts to throb. *Goddamn that hurt.*

It's like hitting him didn't deter him in the slightest. He steps closer to me again and slips one hand up the back of my shirt. "Did that make you feel better?" he taunts me. "Now, kiss it and make it better." He juts his chin toward me, legitimately offering me his jaw like he really thinks I'm going to kiss the slightly reddened spot where I hit him.

"Back off, Jax." I grab his wrist from my back and yank it away, making him let go of me. I'm relieved —but also surprised—when he doesn't fight me more on it.

"You heard her, back off." I'm surprised to see Salma materialize out of nowhere. She rolls her eyes as Jax turns to glare at her, then grabs my arm and pulls me away. I let her do it, because unlike Jax, she doesn't grab my arm like she owns me, she does it in that friendly way people do between friends.

Even as Salma drags me out of the kitchen and into a living room, I can feel eyes on me. Just as she's starting to pull me out the back door, I glance back to find Jax watching me from the opposite side of the room. There's still a darkness in his eyes, but his mouth is curled up in that smirk of his. He's impossible to read, and I remind myself that I shouldn't want to anyway. Whatever is on Jax Woods' mind, it's none of my business.

Salma drops my arm as we find a little open spot in the yard. Several people turn to wave at us, but don't come any closer. Salma grins as I frown.

"What's everyone's deal today?"

"Are you serious?" She stares at me like I'm missing something huge. "I knew you were MIA this summer, but I had no idea you were *this* out of the loop. I thought for sure the guys would tell you what's been going on."

"What? Just tell me."

"You're *it* now, Jules. The top of The Patience School food-chain. You've got more money and family history in Patience than anyone else, which means you're the rightful heir to the top of the social hierarchy. Jax sealed the deal at Prom when he put his stamp of approval on it."

"He did? Why?"

Salma twists her mouth and starts to let her eyes wander. She's trying to avoid answering me, probably because we've had plenty of phone calls this summer where she was forced to listen to me bitch about how it felt like everyone was suddenly pushing Jax on me.

"So people are being nice to me because they think I'm the new head bitch now? That's crazy." A few months ago these people wanted nothing to do with me. They kept their distance, not even bothering to get to know me. Obviously, all that shit happened at prom, but I didn't expect that to be a catalyst for something like this. I really just thought everyone would get a good laugh about me being Prom Queen and then someone else would step up and take over the vacancy Kathryn's death and Cece's arrest left.

"Basically, yeah," Salma confirms. Her face morphs into one of horror. "Oh my god, are we still going to be friends?" *What?* "Please don't drop me. This place is painful without any friends, and I really don't want to have to go back to a boarding school either."

"What are you talking about? I'm not going to *drop you*. You're one of my best friends." I eye her sudden panic wearily. I'm so not in the mood for this. Social rankings? So fucking inconsequential. I have real-life problems I'm still struggling to cope with. I don't have the energy to get wrapped up in this too.

"I don't know! It just seems like the kind of thing people do, dropping their friends when they're suddenly the most popular person in the school. You're already in a group with the guys everyone looks up to, so it kind of makes sense that maybe you'd start hanging with those kinds of girls too." She looks so freaking saddened by everything she's saying, even though I would never do what she's describing.

I take deep breaths in and out until I feel a little calmer. I don't want to get wrapped up in food chains or hierarchies or whatever. I just want to finish high school and maybe find some way to get past the fact that my mother once tried to *fucking sell me*. Oh, and also, I want to find my boys. Where the hell are they? I haven't seen any of them since I got here. My eyes take a quick look around, but I don't catch sight of them out here.

Finally, I turn my attention back to Salma. "We're friends. Nothing is going to change that. I'm not going to forget who was shitty to me and who wasn't just because people finally decided to acknowledge that I've got a last name they think is important." I shake my head, still baffled by the weight people in Patience put on our names. "Now give me a hug and calm down. There's a cute guy over there eyeing you, and you're going to be so mad at yourself if you've got nervous hives when you go talk to him."

"What? Where?" She pulls out of my hug to get a good look, her eyes catching on the blonde that's now smiling at her from the edge of the yard.

"Do you mind if I—"

"Go." I give her a little nudge to help her along. If there's one thing I know I can count on, it's that Salma can always be distracted by a cute face. I absolutely adore her and how easily diverted she is. Just another reason why I would never freaking ditch her, especially not for mean girls that never gave me the time of day before now. I hate that she even thought it was a possibility.

I think back on when I first met Salma, and how distant she was from the rest of our class-mates. She got used to being solo. I understand the feeling, and it makes me feel bad for not reassuring her even more than I did. She looks okay now though, her face lighting up as the cute boy plays with a piece of her hair. Definitely flirting. She's certain to be distracted for the rest of the night. Which means now's the perfect time for me to go searching for my own boys. They have to be around here somewhere. They all said they'd be here, otherwise I would have just pretended to come to the party but hid out somewhere else until I could safely go home without raising Pearl's suspicions.

I walk back into the house and make a loop, but I still haven't found a single one of them. A girl I had English with stops me as I'm starting to make a second loop. "Are you looking for the guys?"

"Yeah, have you seen them?"

"They were in the middle of a video game tournament in the basement earlier. Check there," she offers. I tell her thank you before heading in that direction. I saw the basement steps but I just assumed I needed to steer clear. I thought basements at a party were for making out, not for video games.

As I walk down the steps, I realize there's plenty of room for both. A partial wall separates the room into two distinct living spaces. One with the TV where the games are happening, and one that's just an oversized sitting room—only, the couches are being used for a whole hell of a lot more than sitting right now. I'm still scanning the room when I hear footsteps on the stairs behind me. I step to the side to let the person pass.

Instead, a warm body stops next to mine. I glance over, then do a double-take. Jax. Again. God, he really can't take a hint. I open my mouth to tell him to *fuck off* but he tips his head, nodding toward the other side of the stairs. There's a narrow hallway leading to who knows what over there. No one seems interested in that side of the basement, not when all the action is obviously out here.

When I glance back at Jax, he starts walking that way, not even bothering to see if I'm actually following him like he so clearly expects me to. After what happened upstairs—and also the countless other times I've interacted with Jax—I tell myself I shouldn't go anywhere with him. I can't trust him. But I'm still watching him as he glances back once before stepping around the corner.

I have absolutely no excuse for it. I'm weak. I'm curious. And I find my feet following him even though I know I really, really shouldn't.

When I turn the corner after him, I'm greeted by an empty hallway. I get a weird flash of deja vu to last fall, looking for Sadie on the Forresters' yacht. This time, I know better than to start opening doors. I step slowly down the hall until I come upon the one open doorway. Jax's back is to me as I step inside and I don't know what possesses me to do it but... I push the door closed behind me. Closing me in with him.

My eyes widen to take in the view of the room. Every inch of wall space is covered by fish tanks full of exotic looking fish. The tanks glow in the otherwise dark space, casting a brilliant blue glow over everything else—including Jax. I look at him out of the corner of my eye, watching as he admires the fish tanks too.

"What is this?" I ask, the awe in my voice echoing around the small room.

"Allie's parents are really into fish," he deadpans. "It's fucking weird, but this room looks cool as hell, doesn't it?"

"It's stunning," I admit, focusing my attention back on the tanks. Being in here is what I imagine being inside a submarine would be like. The quiet, enclosed space, surrounded by water and wildlife. Except, okay, obviously these fish aren't exactly wildlife, but close enough. This might be the coolest room I've seen in any house in Patience so far.

Jax takes half a step so he forces himself right into my line of vision. "You closed the door." The suggestion in his voice makes my heart stutter, missing a beat or two. *Yeah, why the hell did I close that door, again?* "Juliet."

The quiet way he says my name sends electricity zapping straight to my lady bits. Damn him. And damn me for following him. He takes another step closer, and in this small space it puts him practically right on top of me. I meet his dark eyes, feeling myself melt for him even as I inwardly scream at myself not to do it. *This is a bad idea.*

But then I'm leaning in and he's meeting me halfway and I swear someone might as well just douse us in gasoline right now because it feels like I'm catching fire. Jax slides his hands around my waist and slides them up the back of my shirt. His body heat is too much, but all I can do is press closer.

I must be possessed because I'm clearly no longer in control of my own body.

I shouldn't be doing this. I've got three guys I really care about and this isn't fair to them. But goddammit I can't seem to make my mouth stop moving with his. He tastes like bubblegum. There's not even the slightest bit of alcohol on his breath. *Has he really not been drinking?* I manage to think about that for about half a second before my mind goes blank again. Jax has this way of making me feel so consumed by him that it's all too easy to forget why we shouldn't be doing this.

I have to stop. I have to go find my guys.

I have to stop, now.

Now.

Okay, *now.*

I turn my head to the side, breaking our kiss. I expect this to be like every other time, with Jax having a hard time taking no for an answer, but he steps back, giving me a bit of space. I focus my gaze on the fish tanks, not wanting to look him in the eyes.

"How can you fucking kiss me like that and then act like you don't want this?" I'm so thankful for the lack of lighting so that he can't see the full flush taking over my face. *How, indeed?*

"I didn't mean for that to happen," I say, the words sounding weak even to my own ears. *I didn't mean for that to happen—what a crap excuse that is.* I can feel the weight of his stare and I'm sure he's thinking the same thing. If I didn't mean for it to happen, I had no business being in here in the first place. I knew exactly what I was walking into. And this time no one dragged me anywhere. I followed him all on my own.

I wait for him to say something. Preferably something cruel so that I stop feeling so off-kilter and go back to feeling the way I usually do about him. Of course, the one time I wish he'd be an asshole, he doesn't say a word.

He grabs me by the waist again and kisses me long and hard. Then, he releases me as if it was nothing and storms past, opening the door and leaving without another word. I press my fingers to my lips and simply watch him go. What could I possibly say right now? I'm not entirely sure I know what the fuck just happened.

I stand there alone, trying to gather myself, and watching all these hundreds of fish swimming aimless circles around their tanks. I'm not sure what's worse, envying them, or feeling like maybe I *am* them.

8

"You okay?" Ace nudges me with his elbow.

I smile and nod, knowing if I open my mouth all the sordid details would come spilling out. How my mother tried to sell me to a mobster. How I kissed the hell out of Jax Woods just minutes before finding the guys at the back-to-school party—and then didn't mention anything about it. It takes real effort to hold in the things I'm not telling them, particularly because I feel guilty as hell about it.

I keep trying to convince myself it would just be easier to be upfront, but then I start picturing them asking questions. I don't want to talk about either thing. My habit of attracting shit parents or my undeniable chemistry with Jax. If I don't talk about it, maybe I can pretend none of it's true. Not that it's working so far.

We're outside the school with nearly the entire rest of the senior class, enjoying the last remnants of summer before we go inside to register for classes. I'm perched up on a brick half-wall by the parking lot, Ace standing beside me with his hand resting on my knee. Smith and Patrick are around here somewhere too, but they're on socialization duty right now. Luckily I managed to talk my way right out of that. Everyone can keep acting like I'm the new Kathryn if they want, but there's no way in hell I'm going to start playing into some social mean girl role. I'm sure someone else will step up for that throne eventually.

"J." I stop looking around at all the people milling about and focus my attention on Ace. "You sure you're okay?

"I kissed Jax." *Dammit.*

Ace blinks slowly for a second before he speaks. "Okay."

"Okay? That's all you're going to say?" Ace is by far the calmest of my three guys, but I still expected a little bit more reaction than that. He taps his fingers along my knee as I try to ignore how distracting it feels.

"Something kind of happened over the summer that you don't know about." Ace glances away and I feel my heart drop.

"What?" I whisper, bracing myself. It's not like I can get mad at him if he hooked up with another girl. It would make me a hypocrite. But god, do I really not want to hear those words come out of his mouth.

Ace runs his hand over his freshly cut hair. "Uh, I've been hanging out with the guys. We haven't talked about why I stopped hanging out in the first place, but they've sort of forgiven me for bailing out on them after... you know."

"Oh, well that's good." I don't know why he sounds so solemn about it. That's great news. I'm glad they're rekindling their friendship.

"We've been talking a lot about you." He blows out a long breath. *Oh.* I gesture for him to go on, even though I'm not so sure I want him to. What if he really is about to tell me something bad? Like the three of them got together and decided I'm not all that great after all. That I don't even deserve one of them, much less all three of them. *He wouldn't be standing here with his hand stroking your leg if that was the case, idiot.* My inner voice really isn't pulling any punches today.

"What about?" I prompt when he doesn't continue right away.

"Mostly about how it's all supposed to work, this arrangement of ours. Everyone is happy with you..." *Well that's a fucking relief.* "But we've all been trying to figure out how to make it work with each other. None of us wanting to be fighting and shit." *I'm still not seeing the problem.* "And, uh, when I say 'the guys' I'm including Jax." *There it is.*

"What do you mean you're including Jax?" I slide down off the wall, forcing Ace's hand off of me. This is one hell of a curveball he just threw.

Ace rubs a hand over his face. I wonder if the other guys put him up to telling me, knowing it would be harder for me to get mad at Ace than the others. There's something about Ace that makes it hard to raise your voice at him, a vulnerability that makes you want to protect him even from yourself.

"It feels inevitable, J. I know you two have a lot of things you're still working out, but no one misses the way you look at each other." His nose wrinkles, and any other time I would take a second to appreciate how cute that is, but dang I'm kind of irritated with him right now. "We all feel better knowing the score. And if it makes you feel any better, I don't see any problems with it. Jax hasn't caused any issues between anyone. If anything, he's been a hell of a lot less of an asshole since we've included him in the conversations."

"I do *not* look at him." Much. Jesus, I do though, don't I? I can't help myself. I must be a masochist because it makes no goddamn sense.

Ace raises an eyebrow and shakes his head at me, though it's more teasing than annoyed. "Is that really all you took away just now?"

"I'm processing," I admit. "Don't rush me."

"I wouldn't dream of it," he tells me with a soft laugh.

The crowd starts to disperse as the doors to the school finally open. I'm not in any hurry to get in there and wait in line for anything, so I stay put and so does Ace. After a minute, Patrick and Smith wander back in our direction. Jax is nowhere to be found, which I'm thankful for. After what Ace just told me, I feel like I have a lot of shit to process before I'm ready to face him again. I keep telling myself he's an asshole and that I should want nothing to do with him. That would definitely be the easy answer. But I have to wonder what everyone else sees that I don't. If the guys were that open to including him this summer—maybe I'm the one who's not seeing things clearly? And that was one hell of a kiss we had the other day. I'm just not sure I'm ready to even give Jax a chance when he's shown zero remorse for how he's treated me.

The other guys? They've all apologized for their bullshit. But not Jax. Jax somehow just always ends up adding more fuel to the fire.

"There's Salma," Patrick says. I turn to follow the direction his finger is pointing and see her climbing out the passenger side of an unfamiliar car. I wondered why she wasn't here yet. I take a few steps forward, planning to walk out into the parking lot to meet her, but I stop short when a guy climbs out of the driver's side.

For a second, I wonder why she didn't mention having a new guy. Then, she looks over at him and even from here I can tell she's smarting off at him. *Definitely not a new love interest.* In fact, as they draw closer, I realize they look a little similar in the face. Salma's barely come to a stop in front of our little group before she's exaggerating a pout.

"My parents made my brother come to pay my class fees." Both my eyebrows shoot up. Salma has a serious spending limit on her credit card, I'm not sure why she'd need him. She rolls her eyes. "I may have gone a tad bit overboard when I spent that week in Spain. Now I'm being punished like a third world citizen." I snort. That couldn't be further from the truth as she stands there decked out in designer clothes after pulling up in a car probably worth enough to feed a third world country for a year. "Anyway," she continues, gesturing to the guy beside her "this is—"

"Kareem," he interrupts her to introduce himself, his voice smooth like butter. He doesn't even bother acknowledging the guys as he leans past Salma to hold his hand out to me. I shake his hand reluctantly, already uneasy from the way Smith just tensed beside me. I start to pull my hand back, even more unsettled when Kareem hesitates before letting go.

Trying to brush off that weirdness, I focus on Salma. "We waited to go in because everyone was rushing in at once."

"Fine by me." She shrugs. She glances around at the guys, her face nothing but polite as she greets the three of them. "Sorry I didn't spend more time with you all at Allie's party. I'm sure you all really missed me," she jokes, batting her eyelashes.

"Oh, trust me, we saw how otherwise *occupied* you were." Patrick grins. He loves giving her shit I've discovered. The two of them have really hit it off with an easy friendship. I was a little jealous at first, mostly because Patrick and I have had a harder time bonding than I have with Smith or Ace, but I'm really glad for Salma's sake that they're getting along so well. She needs the friends, and especially friends that aren't trying to sleep with her.

My gaze slides to Kareem, curious to know how he's reacting to that insinuation about his sister's exploits. I'm surprised to find his eyes on me. Not just casually, either. His stare is *intense*.

I look away, trying to follow the conversation still carrying on around us, but now it's like I can feel his stare. It's jarring. Way more so than when I felt Jax staring at me the other night. My lips pull down into a deep frown as I make eye contact with him again. He looks like he's fighting back a smile, himself.

Salma catches my frown and turns slightly to see what's causing it. Immediately, her eyes lock on her brother. She smacks him with the back of her hand. "Stop staring at my friend. You're being a creep."

He barely flickers his eyes in her direction before he's studying me again. "I just appreciate a good thing when I see it."

I can see Patrick's chest puff out from the corner of my eye. "Stay in your lane, dude."

"You the boyfriend?" Kareem looks at him, seeming to size him up. He must decide he's not too bothered by Patrick's posturing because his eyes are right back on me again.

"Seriously, stop." Salma smacks him again. "They're all her boyfriends, jackass. You're outnumbered."

I can feel a flush creep up my neck as she makes that little announcement so casually. Salma obviously knows what's going on with my dating life, but it's not exactly common knowledge. I fight with myself not to look to see if anyone's around to hear us. I know the news is going to come out eventually, but right now it's just another thing that I'm not ready to deal with yet.

Kareem lets out a long whistle as he eyes all three of my guys. When he centers his gaze on me again, he's smirking, not looking the least bit bothered.

"I'm not intimidated," he tells me as if they aren't standing right freaking here.

"And I'm not interested," I shoot back.

"I like a challenge."

"Still not interested." I frown and turn to the guys, not wanting to play this game of verbal volleyball any longer. They all look pissed. Not that I blame him. Luckily, none of it is directed towards me. They're only glaring at Kareem, who's still wearing that haughty smirk. I'm not interested in stroking anyone's ego.

"What the fuck's going on?" a voice cuts in.

Jax.

There's a dangerous look in his eyes as he sizes up Kareem. I'm not sure how much of that he just heard and I don't want to wait to find out. Jax has a temper, and right now he does not look happy. "Jax," I bite out, forcing his attention to me, instead. "Don't."

"It's okay, beautiful. I can take whatever your boyfriends want to dish out." Kareem winks at me. "Might want to warn you though, buddy," he looks at Jax, "You could hit me in the face and give me black eyes so bad my eyes swell shut, but I'd just take that as an excuse to check your girl out with my hands, instead."

"Shit." The word is barely out of my mouth before Jax grabs a fistful of Kareem's shirt, getting right up in his face as his whole body seems to go red with rage.

There's no time to think, only to react. I jump right in, shoving myself between the two of them and then shoving Jax back as hard as I can. I can feel him tense up, weighing his options, but he lets go of Kareem's shirt and lets me walk him backward until there's several feet of distance between them.

"God, with an ass like that I guess I'd be protective, too." Kareem whistles again, louder this time, like he's really trying to rub it in that he's looking.

I have to close my eyes and take a deep breath before I murder this guy. I feel Jax's chest tense under my hands but my eyes pop open and I shake my head. "Nuh-uh. He's just trying to keep getting a rise out of you," I warn him. "Don't fall for it."

Salma, who's been growing more upset by the second, finally snaps. She pulls back her hand and smacks Kareem right across the face. I turn just in time to see it. He winces from the impact, rubbing his jaw as she scowls at him. She says something quietly to him so that I can't hear, but based on her face I can tell they're angry words. Kareem tries to look up at me again, but Salma throws her fist at his stomach.

"Go!" she shouts in his face, and that's plenty loud enough for the rest of us to hear. She points toward the door to the school. Turning to us, she says, "He's going to go pay for my shit and then leave. I am *so* sorry about him, Jules. I had no idea he was going to be such an asshole." She looks at me hesitantly, almost like she's worried I'm going to send her away with him.

"It's not your fault your brother's a creep. Don't worry about it." I wave off her concern.

It's crazy how a girl with so much confidence and self-assurance could turn so insecure when it comes to our friendship. I swear, at some point she's gonna have to realize that we're solid. If I haven't burned bridges with Sadie yet—whose friendship with me is in way worse shape right now—then Salma has nothing to worry about. Especially when it's seriously not her fault.

"Can we just get this shit over with?" Jax asks from beside me, his voice coming out raspy. I look over at him, but he won't meet my eye.

Everyone mutters their agreement, the mood totally trashed after what just happened. We manage to make it through the rest of registration relatively unscathed. We only run into Kareem one time when he brings Salma a receipt she needs from him paying her school fees. He's staring again, but at least this time he keeps his mouth shut. After that, he bails out, leaving Salma with us after I reassure her I'll give her a ride.

Even after he's gone, I notice Jax sticks close to my side. He's like a bodyguard I didn't want, but I don't say anything because I can tell he's still on edge after what happened outside. I hate that I even care, but here I am. Being considerate of his feelings because I'm a goddamn glutton for punishment.

"Are you okay?" Ace asks after registration closes and before we all part ways again. I can't help but laugh. After all that drama, here we are right back where this day started. I look at where the others are walking slightly ahead of us, watching the easy way they talk and laugh with each other. I don't know what I'd do without these people. Even Jax fucking Woods, though I'd never admit that aloud.

"You know what?" I tell Ace, "Yeah, I think I'm gonna be okay."

9

Most of the first day back to school is a blur. I start feeling myself shutting down less than halfway through the day because of the sheer amount of attention I'm getting. Lunch turns out to be by far the worst because everyone seems to think that's their chance to snatch a minute of my time. I'm not sure why anyone would want to be the top of the social pyramid—it's fucking exhausting.

It's all stupid shit, too. People asking where I went this summer and then acting like I'm being trendy or something when I say I didn't travel. Asking me things about my hometown and then treating my answer like a novelty item. Sticking my words on a pedestal as if these aren't the same kind of things that made people treat me like a social pariah when I first moved to Patience.

What a fucking difference a year makes.

After lunch, I finally get some much-needed

relief. I have Advanced Photography with Ace, and even though the class is made up of all seniors, they're the sub-species of Patience students that care more about being artsy than being popular. A couple of people still try to chat me up, but then the teacher hands us our first assignment, sending us off on our own with the school grounds as our own personal playground now that we're seniors.

Ace and I wander outside since the weather is nice. While lots of other people head out to the courtyard, we go the opposite direction towards the parking lot.

"Hey, where's your car?" I ask, scanning the parking lot. He met us inside this morning, so I didn't see him pull up.

With a grin, Ace takes a set of keys from his pocket and fools with them until a beep sounds from a couple rows over. I look over to see a vehicle lighting up but it's not the one I expect.

"Oh my god, shut up! Is that yours?"

It's a truck. One of only two in the parking lot. Not that it's any less expensive looking than any of the other cars in the lot. Its blue exterior is sparkling in the afternoon sun, drawing me in like a moth to a flame.

"I got tired of you making fun of me," he teases as I peek in the windows to check out the interior.

"Hey! It's not my fault you looked like Hulk driving a clown car." I stick my tongue out at him as I run my hand over the length of his truck, walking my way down to the tailgate. I don't miss the way his eyes track my movement. Suddenly, touching his truck feels way more suggestive than I anticipated.

I pull my hand back, but only so I can unlatch his tailgate and hop on, sitting with my feet dangling over the ledge. Ace studies me, so I study him back. I like the way his green eyes stay so soft, contrasting with the hard lines of his face. Despite his size, there's something inherently gentle about him, something you can see in the way he's careful about the way he moves. He keeps his shoulders relaxed— never intimidating. And when he moves, he's graceful, never bowling people over and pushing his way through a crowd. People move for him when they see him, but it's so, so obvious that he never expects them to.

Ace starts to lift the camera from around his neck as if to take a picture of me. A churning starts in my gut as I look away from him, turning my head to the side to ruin the picture he was about to take.

"J..." I can hear it in his voice he's about to apologize yet again for something I like to think we've mostly moved on from. I hold a hand up to stop him.

"I know you're sorry, Ace. I do." Emotion wells up like a hard knot in my throat. I want so badly to be past this. To be able to smile for his pictures and never even think about the time when he was taking them to hurt me. I know why he did it, I get protecting himself and his friends from the bullshit that happened with Cece, but I still can't forget that protecting them turned me into a casualty.

I spent so much time trying to keep my head above water after those pictures that I never got time to really work through how I felt about being exposed like that. But now, with Ace's camera pointed towards me, it's *all* I can think about.

I hear it smash before I see it. When I turn my head back, Ace's camera is dumped on the ground and his back is to me. He paces several steps away, his fingers laced behind the back of his head. This is probably about as close to him losing his temper as I've ever seen. I clasp my hands in my lap, not really sure exactly what I should do. I'm sure as hell not going to console him for being upset over doing something shitty to me. I've been far more understanding than any reasonable person would ever be.

Just because I understand why he did it, doesn't mean I think it's okay. If the two of us have any hope of making it, we've both got to be able to accept this as part of our history. I'm doing what I can to understand that what he did is not the person he is, but now he needs to come to terms with that too.

"It's so fucked up," he croaks out, his back still turned. "I picture you, and I picture you in that red fucking bra. I shouldn't even know what that looks like—no one should. And it sure as hell shouldn't be the mental image I fantasize to when I think about..." He chokes on his words like he didn't quite mean to get that close to admitting what I can guess was coming next.

He thinks about me, which I like. He pictures me in the underwear set I *burned* last year, which I don't. He's right. This is so fucked up.

"Ace." He doesn't respond. "Ace, turn around."

Slowly, he does what I've asked. I almost wish I hadn't, seeing the anguish on his face. I honestly had no idea this was still eating him up so badly. He might actually be hurting over what happened more than I am. God, I should have known our brief talk over Spring Break wouldn't cut it. This shit isn't resolved for either of us.

"Come here." I hold my hand out to him, curling my fingers to beckon him closer.

He drags his feet coming closer to me. I don't even know what I'm going to do or say until he's standing right in front of me, both of his hands clasped in mine. He looks at me expectantly, something I savor because I know he's letting me lead the way. He cares that I feel comfortable and safe, even if it means stepping back and letting me make decisions for the both of us. Ace respects me.

"Ace," I say his name again, using his hands to tug him down to me. He's so goddamn tall. I wait until we're as close and face-to-face as humanly possible before I say my piece. "When we're ready to take that step for real, you're never going to think about red panties again." My voice comes out so husky I almost don't even realize it's me talking. *Well, shit. That wasn't at all what I meant to say.*

Ace sucks in a sharp breath and I swear I feel the second his hands start sweating. Looks like I surprised both of us.

"Hey!" *Who the fuck is seriously interrupting us right now?* Ace looks over his shoulder as I lean to peek around him. It's a girl from our class—Emery, I think her name is. "Oh." She stops short when she sees me. "I—Uh, I—Sorry?" she stammers, obviously not quite sure what she wants to say. "Mr. Bridges asked me to let everyone know we've only got about fifteen minutes left of class." She looks specifically at me as she adds, "I'm seriously so sorry. I had no idea it was you. I swear I won't say anything." She's wide-eyed waiting for my response but I have no idea what she's so worked up about.

Quietly, for my ears only, Ace says, "She thinks you're out here cheating on Smith with me." *Well, double shit.*

This is a no-win situation for me. Emery can promise whatever she likes, but I know the way gossip works around here. It spreads like wildfire. And with my new unwelcome social status, she's sure as hell going to tell somebody what she saw and then it will only spread from there. I heave a sigh, knowing the only real choice I have is the truth.

"We're not sneaking around. We're dating." I don't offer up anything more than that. Her face twists in confusion. Everyone still thinks I'm just dating Smith. If they suspect anything's going on with Patrick or Ace, they sure as hell don't mention it to me, and the guys haven't mentioned anything either. That's probably all about to change now. *I fucking hate having people all up in my business.*

"Oh, I thought you were dating—"

"I am," I cut her off, my tone making it clear that this is the last of our conversation. "Thanks for the head's up about the time, Emery. See you around." I'm careful to meet her eyes and not show a bit of hesitation. I want to make it clear right from the start that I have nothing to explain and nothing to be ashamed of. Maybe if I set that precedent now, the fallout won't hit quite so hard. *Ha, keep dreaming, me.*

She's quick to back off, nodding and smiling. "Great, see you all later." I hear the strain in her voice and I can tell she's already dying to tell someone what I just disclosed. I'm so fucking glad this day is almost over. Coming out of the closet about having multiple boyfriends was not exactly how I planned to spend my first day back to school.

There is one silver lining, though. This is going to be one hell of a first day back story for Pearl when I get home. Before I left this morning, she told me if I didn't bring an interesting story about my day home that she was sending my ass back out the door. I would certainly say this qualifies.

When Emery's gone, Ace looks at me and shakes his head. "You didn't have to do that, you know," he tells me. "I wouldn't have been mad if you'd wanted to lie. I know this isn't… traditional."

"I'm not going to lie," I return immediately. I've had enough lies for one lifetime, I'm not about to start creating more. "Ace, who the fuck here has room to judge? We live in a town where teenage girls go drinking at the country club to pick up their classmate's married dads. A town where adult women can't be trusted with their teenage kids' friends. And just at this last party, I saw people having straight up threesomes in the middle of the living room. Fully nude. In front of everyone. Anyone who can deal with that shit but not this can just fuck right off, as far as I'm concerned."

His eyes go wide while I'm speaking, but the second I'm quiet they soften back to that familiar look I love so much. When he looks at me like this, this is when I know without a doubt that I can get past what he did with those pictures. I could get past almost anything when he looks at me like this.

"For someone that says they don't want to run things around here, you're pretty damn good at doing just that," Ace says, giving me verbal whiplash.

"What? What do you mean?"

"You just *handled* that girl like a pro. And now here you are telling me you'd rather break the status quo than conform to it. It's pretty badass, and it's a pretty good sign that you're already good at this, whether you like it or not. It's in your blood."

I wrinkle my nose as I push him away—not hard,

I just want some distance after what he just said. "I think the only thing in my blood is chaos."

He tilts his head as he looks at me. "That's got nothing to do with your blood, J. That's just life." I'm not sure truer words have ever been spoken. I remember what Ace has been through. And what Smith goes through with his mom and Sadie being addicts and his dad being absent. And Patrick, with the insane amount of pressure he feels from his parents. And Jax—whose issues I don't quite know yet, though my guess is they've got something to do with his dad.

I think about Nikon Park too. Everyone there comes with an entirely different set of issues. Poverty. Drugs. Gangs. No one comes out unscathed.

"You know," I tell him, "I think that might be the most important thing anyone's said to me all year." Because it's *not* just me. Everyone I've ever met is going through their own shit. Which brings us back to… "Ace, we need to resolve this picture issue once and for all."

"How?"

I don't have a good answer for him. Hell, I'm not even sure if it's actually possible. But I'm a fan of the fake-it-until-you-make-it theory. *So what if we just face it head on instead of hiding from it?* I glance at his abandoned camera, noting with a wince the cracked lens I can see even from over here. He's going to have to get a new one.

I work the strap of my own camera over my head and hold it out to him, nearly laughing when he recoils from it like it might bite him. "Let's fight pictures with pictures." Maybe it will work, maybe it won't. Either way, this is something that doesn't hurt anybody that we can do right here, right now.

"What do you mean?" He frowns, still not taking the camera. I thrust it against his chest and let go, leaving him with no choice but to take it from me or risk my camera being broken, too.

Instead of answering him, I jump down off the tailgate and go around to the driver's side of his truck. I pull the door open, not bothering to wait and make sure any of this is okay, and climb in. I don't move over—he's not getting in. It takes him a second, but he comes to stand in the open space between the door and the truck.

"What are you doing?" he asks, eyeing my warily as I untuck my uniform shirt.

"Changing the fantasy."

Ace looks from me to the school building with alarm as I start to unbutton my shirt. This isn't a striptease, so I don't bother taking my time. We don't have much time left, anyway. Five minutes maybe, tops. I'm not interested in getting caught half undressed in the school parking lot, so once my shirt's unbuttoned I leave it hanging open—that way if someone comes I can cover myself up quick.

"Take my picture," I murmur, sitting up straight as I tuck my loose hair behind my ear on one side.

He stares at me, not moving at all, just his eyes on me like he can't look away. I'm in a simple white lace bra this time, nothing like the red bra that half the town has seen pictures of me in. This time, this view, and these pictures, this is just for him. A symbol of the trust and relationship we're building.

I shift to get more comfortable on the seat and Ace lets out a short groan. "Jesus, Juliet. This is..." He clears his throat. "This is not what I had in mind."

"Take the picture, Ace. I trust you." We fall into a weird kind of staring contest. I think he's trying to call my bluff, but if so he's going to be sorely disappointed. This is no bluff. This is me doing what I should have done a long time ago. Showing him that we don't have to be trapped in the past. If I'd been unwilling to forgive him, I never would have taken him to Nikon Park, or asked him to take me to prom, or any of the other dozens of things we've done together.

It's time to move on, once and for all. These pictures can be the start of a new chapter. It doesn't have to make sense to anyone else, it only has to make sense to us.

As the clock ticks down the minutes until the period is over, Ace finally raises the camera to his eye. His movements are jerky and still uncertain, but now it feels like at least we're on the same page. He points the lens on my camera at me and clicks just once before he's lowering it again. I would have stayed here and let him take as many as he wanted, but I'll accept one as progress.

"I don't see how this is supposed to fix anything," he admits as I hastily re-button my shirt and climb out of the truck to join him.

"Look," I tell him, not even needing to see the picture to know what I'm going to find. I tap the screen and lean in so that we can look at the same time. It's exactly like I thought it would be. "Look at the difference. Think about what it proves."

He studies the photo, and I know he's a talented enough photographer to notice the same things I do. The way my eyes are the focus of this photo, not my body. In those photos he took for Jax, it wasn't about taking a picture of *me*, it was about taking a picture of my body, and this is the exact opposite. This picture is sexy, but not dehumanizing. It looks like the picture of someone worshipping me, not over-sexualizing me. And it's the only proof I need to know we've both passed the one roadblock that was standing in our way of moving forward.

Ace reaches around me to put my camera down on the seat of his truck before putting his arms around me. "I love you, J." The words are quiet, so much so that I'm almost worried I imagined them. But then Ace is looking down at me with more affection than I ever thought I would deserve, and I know I didn't just imagine it.

"I love you, too," I tell him without hesitation.

I can't even stop to consider it's too soon,

because I know in my heart we started building towards this right from that first night I arrived in Patience. When he was just a boy in the dark letting me share his silence. He comforted me then, just by being there, and then he became the first person to start opening up to me. The mess with him and Jax and the pictures was a real shitshow, but everything since has been Ace proving that's not the guy he is.

"You don't have to say it if you're not ready." He looks nervous, like he's not sure I really mean it. So, I repeat myself.

"I love you too, Ace."

Relief floods his eyes as he cups my face in his gigantic hands and kisses me firmly on the mouth. It's not so hard it hurts by any means, but it's the most intensely we've ever kissed. It's like the first time, he's kissing me like he wants to claim me, and I'm sure as hell okay with that.

He only pulls away when we hear the faint sound of the school bell, warning us this period is over. I step aside while Ace locks his car back up, and then he takes my hand and we stroll side-by-side back into school, ignoring the few stray stares as we head towards the cafeteria where all the seniors have to meet for Senior Study Hall. This is the only class we all share. All four guys, Salma, and even Sadie— who's home now, and tentatively speaking to me, though things between us are still awkward.

As we find the others and grab a table together, there's a little bit of guilt lingering in the back of my mind, knowing I've now told Ace I love him when I haven't given the same to my other guys. But I've fallen so hard for all three of my guys, it won't be long before I'm taking the same leap with Smith and Patrick.

Jax is the last to show up. He stops at the end of our table, standing across from me even though the only two open seats are on the opposite side of the table. His eyes flicker from mine down to my chest and then do a bit of a double-take. I blush as I glance down and realize what he's looking at. I missed a button when I was buttoning my shirt, so there's a spot gaping open in my top. From his vantage point, I'm sure he's getting an eyeful of my bra.

On instinct alone, I glance next to me to Ace, and when I look back, Jax glances over at him too. It doesn't take much to practically see the gears turning in his head as I'm sure he takes a guess as to what happened. After the way Jax has acted lately, I'm almost expecting to see jealousy in his expression.

But, no. That's not it at all. The only thing I see as he keeps his eyes on me as he walks to the other end of the table is a heady dose of desire. The kind of desire that makes me sink down in my seat as I discreetly rub my thighs together under the table. *Jax fucking Woods is a real guilty pleasure.*

10

"Remind me again why I decided to do this?" Salma groans.

I pretend to think about it. "Because you crave social acceptance and wanted a chance to hang out with Emmett again in an environment where you can personally guarantee the cleanliness of the bedrooms?"

"You wound me." She gasps and clutches her chest. "Damn, you know me so well. It's like we've been friends for forever." She reaches out to give my hand a quick squeeze. She's been a lot less concerned about our friendship since Sadie's been back. I think because she sees now I'm not just going to bail on her for Sadie just because I was friends with Sadie first. "Hey, I'm gonna do one last check of the pool house. Could you finish this?"

"Sure." I nod, eyeing the last case of drinks that

need to be stuffed into the fridge. It won't take long at all, so I wave her away.

I'm about halfway through the pack when heavy footsteps join me. I nearly hit my head on the refrigerator door when I hear that goddamn familiar whistle. *Seriously?* Salma swore Kareem had plans with his own friends and wouldn't want to hang around here with a bunch of high schoolers all night.

"Let me help," he says, his head of dark, curly hair appearing in my peripheral as he leans down to pick up the case of drinks I'm working on. He shoots me a bright white smile as he stands and hands me one of the cans out of the case. Reluctantly, I take it from him, pulling away quickly when his fingers brush against mine.

"You did that on purpose," I accuse, narrowing my eyes to look at him.

"Abso-fucking-lutely, I did." He smiles wider. He's fucking shameless—and not in a cute way. There's something off about the way he pays attention to me. Like he's not just checking me out, but also looking for weaknesses to exploit. It creeps me out.

Knowing he's not going to go anywhere anytime soon, I make quick work of finishing with stocking the fridge. I'm just loading the last two cans when several more sets of footsteps enter the kitchen. I can feel the energy of the room change, dread seeping in as I can already guess that it's the guys. I told them to show up before everyone else started to, that way I wouldn't be stuck looking for them later in the crowd. *Fuck, if only they'd been like two minutes later.*

"This looks cozy." Patrick sounds pissed. What a perfect way to start the night.

I slam the cans down on the fridge shelf harder than I mean to and turn on my heel. Patrick, Smith, and Ace are all standing there looking like this is about to turn into another showdown. I thank the universe that Jax isn't here, because I don't think I could handle trying again to keep him from swinging at Kareem.

Salma walks in then, immediately freezing and taking stock of what's happening. "What are you doing here?" she asks her brother. "You said you'd be gone a couple of days. I thought you were flying somewhere with your friends?" There's a panicked quality to her tone, probably because she knows as well as I do that having him here is just asking for trouble. I don't wait to hear Kareem's answer, I stride towards the guys.

"Come on," I tell them, trying to lead them out of the kitchen. Let Salma deal with her pervy creep of a brother. Smith falls into step beside me as Patrick and Ace trail behind us.

"If he's still here and Jax shows up..." Smith grimaces.

I hold my hands up helplessly, taking a play out of Smith's playbook since it's one of his favorite gestures. "It's not like I can demand he leaves his own house. Plus, Salma needs this. Hanging out with us is the most she's fit in since she started school here, I'm not ruining that for her by bailing out on her now. You know if you guys aren't here other people won't stay either."

"That goes for you too now, Jules," he reminds me, but I just roll my eyes. I don't like acknowledging my newfound popularity. I'm hoping if I don't acknowledge it then eventually it will just go away on its own. "I'm sure it'll be fine." He doesn't actually sound so sure of that.

The whole thing is making me uneasy. My only hope is that Salma will maybe manage to run him off on her own, but that hope is quickly dashed when she meets us in the living room with a grim expression. "I swear he's not usually this much of an asshole."

"Great, so I just happen to bring it out in him then." That seems about right. *Lucky me.*

Salma shoots me a small, apologetic smile. "We can cancel if you want. I know you only agreed because we didn't think he would be here." I can tell by the way she's wringing her hands together that she hates the idea, and for that reason alone I know I can't ask her to cancel, even though I'd like nothing more than to do just that. It's like I just told Smith— Salma needs this.

"Are you kidding? It would be a crime to deprive people of seeing you in that dress." She's wearing a sleek, metallic dress she picked up over the summer while she was out traveling to all sorts of exotic places. I know she's almost as excited about that dress as she is about the party.

"Thank you," Salma says emphatically, throwing her arms around me in a tight squeeze.

A couple of hours later, I know for sure I made the right choice. Even though the parties are by far not my favorite thing about Patience, Salma manages to slide into her element. She's a good host, probably because she's the only one to host a party in this town sober. It means she's actually making sure everyone's having a good time, instead of getting shit-faced and letting it turn into a free-for-all.

I hang out on the fringes, letting the boys do their thing while I bounce between them and Salma. People flock to me when I'm with Salma, probably because they realize it's the one time I don't immediately try to get away. It's all for Salma's sake, so that I can force people to finally give her the time of day. Once people talk to her for the first time, they see how great she is all on their own, and then I'm able to sneak away, leaving her to socialize by herself. All she needed was that little bit of help getting people in the room, after that, there's just a quality about her that makes people realize they *want* to have her around. It doesn't take long before it's very obvious she's an outcast no longer.

"I've been watching you." I jump from my spot at the second floor railing, from where I've been watching over things for a few minutes. Kareem leans next to me on the railing. "I see what you're doing for my sister."

"Yeah, well, people just needed an excuse to give her a chance." My eyes search out the guys—Jax in particular, who only got here about thirty minutes ago. "You like creating problems, don't you?"

"Excuse me?" Kareem twists so that he's only half leaning on the railing and facing me.

"I've told you I'm not interested. A better man would take me at my word on that and stop churning up drama." Salma's told me some things about her brother, and what she's told me actually reminds me of Jake's brother, Brandon. They're trouble, and absolute heartbreakers if you make the mistake of letting things get that far. Something I have zero intention of doing. I remember the people Brandon hurt. All too clearly, because Jake and I were always the ones stuck picking up the pieces of whatever chaos Brandon had decided to cause.

Kareem scoots closer, and even though I want to take a step back I force myself to hold my ground, instead. "I don't want to be a better man. I want to be a man who wins." He leans towards me as if to kiss me but I'm quicker than he is. I turn my head as he chuckles. "Oh, c'mon. I've probably got more experience than all your boyfriends combined. I could show you a good time."

"All you've shown me so far is that you're a real asshole. I'm not interested, Kareem. Find someone else to harass." I start to step away but he grabs my waist.

He frowns at me as I grab his hands and squeeze until he lets go. He starts to protest, "Don't—"

"She said she's not interested," Sadie interrupts in a sharp voice. I've never been so happy to see her as I am in this moment. "And now you have an audience." She gestures to the railing, and a quick look verifies that yep, everyone is staring up here now, trying to see what's going on. And I can already see the guys making their way through the crowd towards the stairs. *Shit.*

Kareem puts his hands up like a criminal being stopped by the police. The metaphor feels about right at this particular moment. Shaking my head at him as he just smirks at me, I grab Sadie and make for the stairs.

"Thank you for that. That guy's a real asshole," I mutter.

"Yeah." She glances back. "I don't trust that guy, Jules. You need to be careful not to get stuck anywhere alone with him."

Even the idea of it makes me shudder. "Don't worry, I don't plan on it."

We reach the stairs right as the guys are starting to come up. To my surprise, it's Smith walking in front. All three of my guys are standing in front of Jax, who's standing behind them with a furious expression on his face. *They're blocking him*, I realize. God, I know they're friends, but this feels like something else. This feels like them protecting him as part of *our* group, and I'm not so sure how I feel about that considering all the unresolved issues between Jax and I.

For the moment, it's good they're looking out for him. I know his father gets him out of all kinds of messes, but he needs to stop pushing his luck. Eventually he's going to walk himself right into a mess that daddy can't bail him out of.

"What?" Jax snaps, seeing me staring at him.

"Watch yourself," Smith turns and huffs at him. That's a whole other surprise. It's not often I get to see Smith standing up to Jax. I have to hope that means he's finally ready to start treating Jax like a regular friend instead of an idol.

Jax looks away from the group, and I swear it almost sounds like he mutters a "sorry" under his breath.

"Please don't let that asshole up there ruin everybody's night. Let's go out back. I heard someone mention beer pong." Smith's eyebrows lift. He knows I'm not going to drink. I never do. The one time I slipped up since coming here obviously didn't work out so well for me. I'm not taking any chances a second time. "You all can play. I'll be your designated cheerleader."

There's a little bit of grumbling, but finally everybody agrees. As the guys start to head outside, Sadie touches my shoulder and tells me she thinks she needs to go home. I fall back with her, letting the guys go ahead.

"Are you okay?" I eye her, looking for signs I might have missed that she's been drinking or taking anything. Her icy blue eyes are crystal clear as she nods.

"Yeah, I'm just not sure I can handle anymore tonight." She starts to part ways, but pauses. "Thank you for caring. I haven't had a lot of that." She smiles at me one last time and then she's gone. It makes me feel sorry for her. It's no wonder she's lashed out at me through the process of getting sober. She's used to people turning a blind eye—and I chose not to.

I turn the opposite way from Sadie, following the path the boys took to the backyard. It doesn't take long to find them. They're rowdy as hell over the game already, the scene that just happened inside all but forgotten for the moment. I stand off to the side, enjoying watching them do their thing. A little bit of a crowd starts to gather as word spreads that the guys are locked in what might be the most intense game of beer pong ever played.

They're midway into their rematch when my phone starts to vibrate in my pocket. Anyone who should be calling me is here, which means... I yank the phone out as fast as I can. Jan's name flashes across the screen. I have about four vibrations left I'm guessing before it rolls over to voicemail.

"You guys, this is the nurse. I have to answer it."

All four of them start to follow me. "No, stay. Finish your game. I'll be right back." As they go back to playing, I pick up the call, crossing the yard as quickly as I can so that I can get away from the noise. "Hello?"

"Juliet?"

"Miss Jan? Is everything okay?" My voice wavers, nerves I'm sure coming through clear across the phone line.

"Oh, I sure didn't mean to worry you, dear. You asked me to tell you if your aunt mentioned anything peculiar about her brother Hollis?" She sounds uncertain now, as if she's remembering wrong. It's been weeks since I brought that up.

I nod, then remember she can't see me. "Yeah. Yes. What did she say?"

"Well, I'll admit I think I missed some of it but— Uh, let me check here. I wrote down what I could make of it just in case you didn't answer." She makes a couple of shuffling noises before continuing. "Ah, yes. Here it is. Oh gosh, look at my handwriting." *In about thirty seconds I'm going to wring stand-in Grandma's neck* "Hollis married everything he ever loved." God, I can't believe I let this woman get my hopes up.

"Okay, thanks for letting me know. I don't really think that's probably significant. Pearl was probably just thinking about Hollis' wife." She died before he did. I'm sure he did love her, the pictures of the two of them are all pretty sweet. He used to look at her the way...well, the way I think Patrick looks at me. Like we're partners. Equals.

"No, wait!" More shuffling. "Buried. Hollis *buried* everything he ever loved." That changes fucking everything.

"Are you sure?" I croak out. "She said the word *buried*?"

"Yes. Yes, I'm sure of it now. Is that helpful?"

"Yeah," I tell her. Quietly, mostly to myself, I add, "And also, not at all." Before she can ask any questions, I say goodbye and hang up on her. I don't want to hear anymore.

Hollis buried everything he ever loved. If he buried a treasure, what are the odds anyone ever actually finds it?

"That sounded intense." Kareem's voice makes me jump. Where the fuck did he even come from? I really need him to go back to wherever that was. I'm pretty sure he was in college the last time Salma talked about him, and I'm pretty sure he wasn't graduating, so I'm not sure what it is exactly he's doing here. He should have gone back to school by now.

"Were you eavesdropping on me?"

"Not on purpose." Somehow, I don't quite believe that. At least this time, he's making no move to get into my personal space. Instead, he leans against the exterior wall of the house, his whole body relaxed. Either he's not planning to follow me if I walk away or he's assuming I'm not going anywhere.

Joke's on him. I slide my phone into my back

pocket and start heading back to the party. A few seconds later, I can hear him start to move to follow me. *Dammit.* I look over at him just as he tries to fall into step beside me. I come to a screeching halt. If I walk back around the side of the house with him next to me, it's going to cause problems.

"What part of *not interested* do you not understand?" I frown at him.

"The part where you're the one saying it." His mouth spreads into a wide grin that I'm sure he thinks makes him look more endearing, but it's just further proof that he's trying too hard. There's nothing natural about it. "Oh, c'mon. You're open-minded enough to have a whole harem's worth of boyfriends, but not enough to give a new guy a chance?"

He takes a step closer to me, getting into my personal space again. This guy is a real jackass. "I'd be more than happy to give a new guy a chance—if that guy wasn't *you*."

A flash of anger crosses over his face before he hides it behind another too-wide smile. Now though, I see the way his eyebrow twitches ever so slightly. I managed to get to him, he's just not going to dare let me know it. Hoping it'll be enough to get him to back off, I turn the corner back toward the party. As much as I hate risking more problems with the guys, I don't want Kareem to think he can manipulate me by using that to his advantage to trap me alone. Sure enough, when I risk a glance back, he steps around the corner after me but doesn't follow past that.

Not that it matters. As I rush back across the yard toward my guys, I see them all look past me to where Kareem is standing. No one makes a move in that direction. That's something at least.

"Did that guy just fucking approach you again?" Patrick's voice is a low growl. I've gotten somewhat used to his displays of jealousy, but this is on a whole other level. And because Kareem makes me so uncomfortable, I can't even blame him for it this time.

Reluctantly, I nod. I'm not going to start lying to them about it. "It's fine, I took care of it."

"Are you fucking kidding me?" Jax raises his voice. Whatever they'd done to calm him down before, obviously the spell has worn off. His whole body tenses as he paces a few steps away from the beer pong table. "You all really want to just ignore the way he's openly eye-fucking her from across the yard? This is bullshit. I'm ending this."

He starts to cross the yard fast enough that I barely manage to catch up to him. I yank at t-shirt, sure that I'm stretching it out, and I say his name, trying to force his attention to me instead of Kareem, who's now smirking like he'd be more than happy to go toe-to-toe with Jax. This can't happen. I don't want anyone to get hurt or in trouble, especially not over something as stupid as a guy who can't seem to get it through his skull that his creeper act isn't the slightest bit appealing.

"Jax, stop!" I finally snap at him.

He rounds on me so suddenly that I have too much momentum to stop. I smack into him with an *oomf*. His hands loop around my waist, steadying me as I nearly bounce off of him from the impact. People are starting to stare. But I have to figure, if it's between people talking about this or people starting rumors about an otherwise inevitable fight —I'll take the option where no one ends up bloody or bruised.

"Let's go inside. All of us. Salma showed me how to get into the spare bedroom, we can go there." His eyes flash with expectation as I lose a fight with the blush trying to creep up my neck. "Not like that. Just so that we can take a quiet minute for everyone to chill out."

"Too bad," he murmurs, his teeth skating over his bottom lip.

But he lets me lead him back to the other guys, where I pitch the same idea to them. Soon, they're abandoning their game and following me upstairs, the five of us disappearing into the guest bedroom together.

Yeah, I really should have thought that one through.

11

The rumors are running rampant the next day. If I thought it was bad when people were whispering about me dating two different guys, it's nothing compared to the rumors that start after my class-mates see me disappear into a bedroom at a party with four guys. And not just any four guys either, but the four most well-liked seniors at The Patience School.

Of course, no one comes to say anything directly to me, but by second period on Monday Salma admits she's already had several people ask her if she knows what my deal is. By lunchtime, she confirms the rumors are only growing.

I can't help but wonder if maybe this will be the thing that lets me give up my imaginary Queen Bee crown. That would be one hell of a silver lining.

"Lexington." I've only half turned at the sound of my name before Jax is grabbing me by the elbow. He grabs me hard enough that I wince, dragging me the opposite direction of where I was headed. I just finished Photography with Ace and we're supposed to be heading back to the cafeteria for study hall.

I shoot Ace a confused look as Jax drags me away, but he only shakes his head and shrugs helplessly. He doesn't know where Jax is taking me either.

"Jax, you're gonna make me late," I whine as we get further and further away.

"I got permission for us to study elsewhere." That's hilarious, since he's not carrying a single thing with him to suggest he's planning on studying. I feel my heart-rate skyrocket as I realize where we're going. The study rooms by the library.

I haven't forgotten what happened the last time I was alone with him in one of those rooms. He kissed me on the desk in a way that fucking *ruined me*, and then not long after that he was actually emotionally ruining me. I've got a lot of mixed feelings about these rooms.

I shouldn't go in there with him. Not when I haven't decided what I'm even going to do about Jax. But my brain and my feet are on two very different pages. My feet don't so much as hesitate as Jax pulls me into one of the rooms—the same one he kissed me in —and slams the door shut behind us. There's a serious feeling of deja vu as he backs me against the desk and then lifts me so I'm sitting on the edge of it. He steps in between my legs and I swear to god my lips part for him all on their own.

He raises an eyebrow. "I didn't bring you in here to grope you." He looks down at my bare legs as he drops his hands on my thighs. It's still warm enough I haven't started wearing tights with my uniform. His voice is thicker as he adds, "Though I'm sure it could be arranged.

What the hell is it about this guy that turns me on so freaking much? I'm trying not to forget what an undeniable asshole he's been, but that's harder than I anticipated when his thumbs start rubbing circles on the inside of my thighs.

I have to clear my throat twice before I manage to speak. "Why are we in here then?" His thumbs still.

"People are talking." He studies me as he says the words, but if he's looking for a reaction, I don't have much of one. This isn't news to me. I know people are talking.

"There's nothing I can do about it," I say with a shrug. I hate knowing I'm at the center of the gossip mill, I've hated that since arriving here, but I can't control it. People are going to talk. Especially when I'm doing something they see as so out of the ordinary by openly dating multiple guys.

"That's not even remotely true." He rakes his hands up my thighs until his fingers are clenching the side of my ass. I'm starting to think maybe the touching is a distraction. "There is something you can do. Something that you need to do."

"And that is?"

"When the opportunity comes up—when someone tries to start shit because they're making a play for your spot—you need to shut it down. Hard."

I scoff. That's the exact opposite of what I want. Please, please let someone make a play for my spot. I'm more than happy to willingly hand it over. When I first got here, I thought being ignored was the worst possible thing, but it turns out being the center of everyone's attention is much, much worse. I was never used to that, and I don't want to deal with it now.

"Listen, Princess. You can roll your eyes at me all you want, but you and I both know this is your birthright. What happens when Pearl isn't here anymore? Are you really going to be able to live with yourself if you give up one of the few things she really wanted for you?" I open my mouth to protest but he shakes his head. "The house, the money, and the status—am I wrong?"

Dammit. He's not wrong.

Is this what it means to take ownership of my name? Jax called this my birthright. Am I somehow neglecting the family legacy if I choose to turn my back? And more importantly, do I really want to risk finding that answer out the hard way? If I let myself fall prey to social suicide, there's a good chance there's no coming back. It's easy to say I don't want the attention while I've got it, but what about when it's gone? Am I really Juliet Lexington if I don't take everything that was meant to be mine?

I don't understand the obsession with family names here, but maybe that's only because I haven't taken the time to try. Nearly everyone else seems to think the hierarchy matters. Maybe it's for reasons I just don't understand yet.

"I don't even know how to do what you're telling me to do," I admit.

Jax studies me, searching for sincerity in my eyes. "Your name makes you royalty and that means you choose the law of the land. If someone has something to say, remind them of that. You don't have to be an outright bitch like Kathryn was, but people will respect you if you're firm."

If Jax had been giving me advice even just a few months ago, I would have questioned his intentions. Now though, I suspect he's being honest. Or maybe that's my hormones talking, because it sure is one hell of a distraction trying to listen to him talk as he kneads the sides of my ass with his knuckles.

Patrick might be more popular and well-liked overall, but it's Jax that everyone turns to for social cues. He might be one of the world's biggest assholes, but he knows what he's talking about.

"Okay," I finally say simply.

"Okay?" He looks surprised. Not that I blame him. I'm sure he expected me to fight him a lot more on this. The two of us definitely have a tendency to be oil and water together. It does help his case that in the back of my mind I can't stop thinking about how often this summer I had to listen to everyone telling me to go easier on him and give him a chance. Here's his chance. If this turns out to be some sort of cruel joke, I'll never fucking trust him again.

"Okay," I repeat with a nod. This is his one chance.

He breathes a sigh of relief as he works his hands up and flattens his palms against the small of my back. Something about the gesture immediately rockets me right into the danger zone. I watch my hands run over his chest as if they're attached to someone else. His eyes go hooded as he lets me touch him. This is such a bad idea.

And then we're kissing. There's no easing into it or anything, we're both just suddenly *there*, our mouths fusing in a kiss that's not even remotely appropriate for a school building. He takes his hands off my back so he can tangle them in my hair, tilting my head to the side to get an angle he likes as he leans over me. I feel needy and hot as I shift on the desk, trying to find some relief against the cool wood.

It's amazing that no matter how much I've loathed Jax over the past year, he can still manage to work me up into such a frenzy. It's frustrating and sexy all at once. I have no self-control, dammit.

Jax is the first to pull away, his breathing ragged as if he's just run a marathon. Mine admittedly isn't much better. He turns away for a minute, bending over with his hands on his knees. I open my mouth to ask him if he's okay but before I can get the words out he's on me again, kissing me this time with a frenzy that makes me a little anxious. His hands seem to touch me everywhere at once, lighting a fire in me that I'm not prepared for. By the time he's pushing my skirt up my legs, I almost don't even notice through the haze he's caused to my brain.

"What are you doing?" I break our kiss and push my skirt back down to cover my underwear.

"I thought—" He steps back, pulling away from me completely. "Forget it," he mutters, reaching down to adjust himself through his pants. My eyes can't help but drop as he does it, and I get one hell of a look at his straining bulge. Only for a second though, before he's yanking the door open.

"Where are you going?" I try to ask, but he's already slamming the door closed back behind him. I have no idea what the hell just happened. Did he really think that I wasn't going to put a stop to that? I'm still not even sure I should be letting myself get caught up in kissing him, much less letting him hit a home-run in the middle of a school day.

I don't understand him. It seemed like he was doing something nice by giving me advice, but was it really just a means to an end? Pretend to care so that he could try to get in my pants? I'm so tired of second-guessing everything with him. Eventually, something's got to give. And I sure as hell don't intend for that something to be my panties.

Not wanting to spend another minute in that tiny box of a room, I start to head back toward the cafeteria where I should have been in the first place. I'm just turning down the main hall when a group of juniors come out of one of the classrooms, their teacher leading them probably to the library, if I had to guess. I don't think anything of it until I'm passing them and get shoulder checked. Any other time, maybe I could ignore it, but Jax's words are still ringing in my ears, whether his intentions were really good or not.

I turn on the blonde girl that bumped me. "Is there a problem?"

Her eyes go wide as she quickly looks to the front of the line. If she's looking for her teacher to save her, she's out of luck. The woman is far enough ahead that she's already turned the corner and is surely out of earshot. She looks back at me and quickly shakes her head. The people around her saw what happened and are now frozen, waiting to see what's going to happen.

It would be over right then if she didn't mutter, "Slut," just loud enough for everyone to hear.

"Because if there was a problem," I continue as if she hadn't said anything, "it would be with *you*, not me. I mean what kind of girl worries about what another girl's got going on in the bedroom?" I glance to the girl standing closest to us. "That's just sad, wouldn't you agree?"

"Yeah," the bystander agrees emphatically.

The girl that shoulder bumped me looks positively green now. It's more than obvious that she thought she was going to get to be an asshole and not get called out for it. She glances around and I know she sees the same thing I do, not one of these people is willing to stand up for her. In fact, they've all but shuffled slightly further to the side, as if afraid of being guilty by association.

"Sorry I bumped you. It was an *accident.* There's no problem." The girl's words sound insanely robotic, but it's clear she's making the choice to back down. *I can't believe that actually fucking worked,* I think to myself.

"Great. See you around," I say pointedly as I continue down the hall like I wanted to in the first place.

I have a lot of mixed feelings running through me as I enter and take my seat with the crew—minus Jax —in the cafeteria. I want to feel good knowing I stood up for myself, but I can't help feeling bad for embarrassing someone like that. Sure, I wasn't nearly as mean about it as Kathryn or Cece would have been, but I'm still not sure I really did the right thing. I don't want to be a mean girl. Especially not when the idea of it just make me replay the words Jake said when he left me at my birthday party.

"You're different here, and I don't think it's in a good way."

Even though we haven't talked in months, and even though I know he betrayed my trust to the woman I once thought was my mom, I can't help the lingering part of me that still cares what he would think of me. He would never have wanted me to be a pushover. He always gave me shit about being too nice at home. But there's a fine line between sticking up for yourself and putting other people down—and I don't know that I actually know where that line is.

Smith's hand finds my knee under the cafeteria table. "What's wrong?" he asks quietly enough that the others can't hear him. Even though this is supposed to be study hall, it tends to be loud as hell in here. That's what happens when you put an entire class of seniors in one big room and tell them to prepare themselves for college.

"I'm afraid of losing myself." It terrifies me to say the words out loud, as if somehow that will make the prospect more real. If I don't say it, acknowledge it out loud, I'm worried I'll lose myself without ever even stopping to notice.

"What makes you say that?"

Salma, who's sitting right across from him, tunes in as I start explaining what just happened in the hall. I even mention Jax's advice, though I leave out the other details of what happened in the study room. It feels like I'm protecting him by not saying anything, though I can't for the life of me under-stand why I care. It's not like he deserves my protec-tion—or even really needs it, for that matter.

"I don't know what to say," Smith admits.

"I do—or rather, I know who does." Salma stands up as the end of the day bell chimes and beckons me to follow. I go along with her, even though I'm not sure what she's got up her sleeve. I'm a little surprised when all she does is to take me to the women's restroom in the main hallway. Usually we avoid this one because it gets so crowded.

With eyebrows furrowed, I follow her into the empty bathroom. Thanks to Salma's speed walking, we're the first ones in here. I open my mouth to ask what's going on, but the words disappear into thin air as Salma tugs me into one of the stalls with her.

"What—" This feels like it's about to turn into a bad porno or something.

Salma shushes me and holds a finger over her lips. The universal sign for *be quiet*. I watch with horror rolling through me as she steps up onto the toilet seat and crouches. What the hell? It takes me a second to realize she's probably trying to hide the fact that there's two of us in here.

"Salma, what are we doing?" I whisper. She just shushes me again.

Maybe a minute passes before the bathroom door creaks open and I can hear a flood of girls coming in. They sound like they're all trying to talk at once, but after another minute it finally calms down a little so that I can make out bits and pieces of conversation. It's the least I can do to distract myself from the fact that I'm currently hiding out in a bathroom stall. Rich kids or not, school bathrooms are what nightmares are made of.

"Did you hear what happened to Megan Oliver?"

"Yeah, girl! Can you believe she had the balls to

call Juliet Lexington a slut right to her face? I mean, I knew she was dumb, but that's some next level shit."

"Social suicide, for sure."

"Don't tell me you feel bad for Megan, of all people?"

My heart squeezes in my chest. This is it, confirmation that I've turned into an unlikable bitch instead of an unlikeable outsider. I cover my eyes with my hands, as if that could somehow block out all the shit I'm sure I'm about to hear about myself.

"Hell no, I don't. Apparently, after Juliet handed her ass to her, Megan ended up apologizing to those two freshman she was bullying the hell out of. She's terrified now that Juliet's going to send her to social purgatory, so she's actually being fucking nice to people for once. I was already on Team Lexington anyway, but now I'm double sure that she's the one that should be leading things."

Oh. *Oh.* That is not even remotely what I expected to hear. I uncover my face, only to see Salma with a big ass grin on her face as she watches me while I listen.

"God, can you imagine if Kathryn were still around?"

"Yeah, Megan would have been shit out of luck. This way, at least she sort of gets a chance to clean up her shit." There's a lull in the conversation as someone turns the water on full blast. "Fuck, it's too bad we didn't have Juliet all along. It's a lot more bearable around here."

"Yeah. Hell, if her only flaw as the new reigning queen around here is that she stole the four hottest guys in school for herself, I think I can live with that."

"I mean, honestly, who can blame her right? Who wouldn't want to date all four of them if we had the chance?"

The two girls burst into laughter that fades away as I listen to them leave the bathroom.

After another minute or two, the bathroom starts to go quiet as everybody leaves for the day. Only after the coast is clear does Salma step down and let us out of the stall. I'm pretty damn thankful for that, since the last thing I need is more rumors floating around. Salma is gorgeous and I adore her, but not like *that*.

"See?" Salma gloats as we both come stumbling out.

I have to admit, "That wasn't what I was expecting."

"You might have seen it as being mean, but other people saw it as you not taking any crap. Now, it's like any of us could have a harem of boys at our beck and call. You gave us that hope," Salma jokes. I shake my head at her even as I laugh a bit myself. There's one thing I still don't understand.

"How did you know to bring me in here?"

"Are you kidding? This is the best place to come to find out what's at the heart of the gossip." She takes her phone out and scrolls to something, then hands it to me. "Plus, I happened to see this probably seconds after you put that girl in your place. So I knew people would be talking about it."

I study her phone screen with a sinking stomach. It's one of those goddamn pictures of me in my underwear. I knew people would have saved the pictures, there's nothing I could do about that, but I didn't think anyone would have the nerve to repost any of them. Especially not on this site, which functions as The Patience School's private discussion board for students.

Salma sees my face and reaches over me to scroll down the screen. "Read the comments," she instructs.

So, I do. I read them all. There are literally hundreds of them already, and at one point I at least let Salma drag me out of the bathroom so that we're standing in the hallway as I scroll. Salma wasn't kidding. People have really stuck up for me and what I did. They're calling me *one of the best things to ever happen to Patience.* That's quite a stretch from starting as the girl no one even wanted to be seen talking to.

"This is insane," I say finally, handing Salma back her phone.

Salma's grin widens. "Juliet, the only thing people around here like more than having a clear leader, is having a leader like *you*."

12

It's a few weeks after the start of school when I come home to find a vaguely familiar car in the driveway. I don't realize why it's so familiar until I'm turning my key in the front lock and a voice coming from Pearl's temporary room drifts out to greet me.

"Someone's going to sell eventually," he says.

There's a break as if he's listening to another person respond. Pearl, I presume, considering the direction the voice is coming from and the fact that her voice has gotten so small these last couple of weeks that it's barely more than a whisper anymore.

The man continues, "I think it's a mistake. It's reckless to think a teenage girl is ready for that kind of responsibility. The amount of property she'll have to deal with alone. How do you not see that it's too much?"

There's another brief moment of quiet before I

hear footsteps. I'm halfway across the entryway myself when Brock Forrester appears in the doorway to the formal sitting room. He freezes in place when he sees me, his eyes doing a slow perusal of me that makes me decidedly uncomfortable. At least with Mr. Forrester, I've seen proof he can take no for an answer, unlike Kareem, who gives me that same uncomfortable vibe. If I had to choose the lesser of two evils, it would definitely be this guy.

"I didn't know we were expecting company," I tell him in lieu of an actual greeting.

Brock glances behind him into Pearl's room before scoffing as he looks back at me. "Your great aunt is a very stubborn woman. When your time comes to make decisions alone about all the property you now own, I hope you'll discuss things with me. Unlike *some people*," —he definitely means Pearl — "I know the value of the Lexington fortune. And sometimes the best value is in selling rather than holding."

I blink at him, completely baffled that he's bringing this up right now. I might now own the Lexington fortune, but I'm not touching any of it so long as Pearl is still kicking. And even then, I'm not sure I could ever go against the wishes of the woman who took me in instead of making me an orphan.

I can't say any of that without being rude though. I give him a noncommittal, "Uh-huh," instead.

Brock looks around us, his eyes scanning the

extravagant entryway of the house in a shrewd kind of way. When his eyes finally fall back to me, there's genuine concern in them. "You need to be careful, Juliet. Pearl's played the gatekeeper here, and now that will fall to you."

"I thought you didn't believe in Hollis' treasure?"

"I don't." His mouth tightens into a thin line. "But other people do. And believing in something that doesn't exist? That's far more dangerous."

He's not wrong. How many times has Pearl had to scare a late-night visitor off because they were convinced they could find Hollis' rumored treasure? While most of them were easily scared off, a few of the more determined ones have made return trips over the last year. None of them have ever been violent or destructive really, but it's not hard to imagine that if someone got desperate enough, they might become both of those things.

"Just keep it in mind," Brock tells me with a half shrug.

He crosses the entryway as if to leave, but I'm not quite done talking. "Hey, can I ask you something?"

He turns back to me. "You always do."

I flush a little bit at the insinuation that I ask too many questions. I'm a curious girl, sure, and my curiosity hasn't always served me well, but I try not to overdo it. There's just something I've always wondered about for a while.

"That first night I met you, at The Patience Club,

Kathryn Lassiter approached you. Why weren't you interested?" The age obviously wasn't the issue, considering his interactions with me and the way his eyes keep flickering to check me out in the most obvious way.

Brock runs a hand over his beard as he genuinely seems to think about my question. "Kathryn Lassiter had a reputation. She might screw you, but she'd also screw you over. Braver men than me faced the consequences of touching her." He shudders like it horrifies him just to think about.

"What about Cece?" I don't know what it is I'm looking for. Answers? Insight? All I know is this is like a train-wreck that I can't stop looking at.

"Cece Winchester?" A shrewd look comes over his face. "I don't know. Most of the men thought she was a little too far up the crazy side of the hot-crazy scale. Personally, it always seemed like an act to me. If a girl seemed crazy enough, a man might make the mistake of thinking she'll miss little details. Like things he says in her company that he otherwise might not have. Do you see what I'm saying?" He raises his eyebrows suggestively.

It's almost like he's suggesting that there's something Cece might have overheard that would matter to me, but I can't imagine what on earth it would be. Damn him for stoking the fire of my natural curiosity. Now, it's going to drive me crazy.

As if anticipating me having more questions, he tells me, "That's really all I've got for you. It shouldn't come as too much of a surprise considering your own background, but people aren't always what they initially seem. Watch your back, Miss Lexington." And with that, he sees himself out, leaving me even more confused than before.

What the hell does Cece know?

13

Yet another party. I'm not sure how many more of these I can stomach. There's only so much time a person can spend entertaining themselves by watching everyone else get drunk. And I'm about tapped out.

It doesn't help that Salma's hosting again since her parents are out of town at some pharmaceutical conference for the weekend. I keep looking over my shoulder, worried her brother is going to show up again. I don't know why I'm so on edge about it, it's already late. If he was going to show up, he surely would have done it by now. Smith and Ace have both already begged off for the night, and I'm pretty sure Patrick will probably be heading out soon, too. The only reason I'm still here is because Pearl demanded I not come home for the night. She's really doubling-down on her demands for me not to hover over her every chance I get.

So, I'm staying with Salma tonight. Another reason to not want Kareem to show up. Salma swears he had plans in NYC, but I remember how it went the last time he had plans.

As if my thoughts alone conjured him, the next time I look up from my spot perched on the armrest of the sofa, Kareem is crossing the room towards me. Patrick, who's on the seat of the couch right next to me, has been resting his hand against my lower back, so he feels the moment I stiffen. Leaning forward to see what's gotten my attention, he lets out a string of curse words that even make me blush.

"This asshole has to be fucking kidding me," he spits out as he stands up and steps in front of me so that I'm partially blocked from view.

"I'm not here to fight," I hear Kareem say. "My sister told me I needed to come apologize if I wanted to be allowed to sleep in my own bed tonight." Patrick doesn't move, and after a second Kareem huffs. "Fuck. Whatever. I'll sleep in the damn car."

I almost let the moment pass without saying anything, but then my conscience kicks in. "Wait." I scramble up off the armrest and step around Patrick. "This is your house. You shouldn't be sleeping in the car." I regret my decision almost immediately when I see the calculated way Kareem smiles at me. *He set me up.* Salma probably doesn't even know he's here.

"I'm getting Jax. Nobody ever questions him. Let him be the one to fucking deck this guy," Patrick grumbles under his breath, stepping away I'm sure to do just that.

"No, Patrick, wait," I try to stop him, but it's too late. He's already halfway across the room before I even finish getting the words out. Yet again, this is going to end up turning into a much bigger deal than it needs to be. I scowl at Kareem. "Why can't you just back off?"

"I'll back off," he says, but I can tell there's more from the way he smirks. "After you spend the night with me."

"I'm not doing that. Not ever." What part of that does he not understand.

"We'll see about that," he says. Warning bells start going off in my head. "Some girls just need more… convincing than others."

Kareem's eyes go wide as he's suddenly dragged backward by the collar of his shirt. "What the fuck is that supposed to mean?" There's rage on Jax's face unlike anything I've ever seen before, and even though it's not directed at me, it scares me. It scares me *for him*. He gives Kareem a good shake, handling him as if he was an unruly toddler instead of a fully-grown man. "If you so much as lay a hand on her," Jax growls, the warning clear.

"Oh, I'm gonna use much more than just my hands," Kareem says with a laugh right in Jax's face. "She looks like the kind of girl that would beg to take it raw, don't you think?" *What a fucking asshole.*

I see the hit coming even before Kareem does. Jax

punches him right in the face, one solid blow that sends blood immediately spurting out of Kareem's nose. It's got to be broken. And after the bullshit Kareem just spewed, I can't even find it in me to feel a little bit bad about it. Jax shakes his hand out, even from here I can see the split skin of his knuckles from how hard he decked him.

"That all you got?" Kareem taunts. "I'd have thought you'd be better with your hands. Maybe it'll be easier to steal your girl than I thought."

This time when Jax starts swinging he doesn't stop. The party around us finally comes to a screeching halt as everyone realizes a full-blown fight is breaking out. Patrick appears by my side, putting himself between me and the fight as best he can as I try to shuffle around him. This has to stop. But when I try to step forward, Patrick yanks me back.

"You're gonna get yourself hurt," he growls at me.

I blink back tears as the two guys fall to the floor, still grappling as they take whatever cheap shots they can at each other. Jax gets an uppercut to Kareem's jaw, but Kareem manages to maneuver so that he returns a hard kick to Jax's gut, knocking the wind out of him for a moment. My whole body shakes as I watch them coat the wood floors with blood.

They're still going as Salma bursts into the room with fury in her eyes. Someone must have told her what was going on because she's barely stepped foot into the room with us before she's dousing them with a big bucket of water she brought with her.

"Both of you fucking stop it!" she shouts at them as they both make another grab for each other.

"Kareem! In ten seconds I'm calling the fucking police." My heart stops, worried about what will happen to Jax, who technically started the fight. I'm surprised when the words draw Kareem to a sudden halt. *He probably has a record*, I realize. No one else would look that concerned about the prospect of the cops being called.

Now that the guys aren't taking swings at each other, Salma drops the bucket and grabs her brother by the shirt. "Out. Right now." She sounds scary even to me, and he follows without another word. He looks back once as she drags him out of the room, but I quickly look away. Fuck him for being so disgusting and creating even more issues than there were before.

It's just Jax now, standing in the middle of the bloody floor, panting to try to catch his breath. He looks up, seeming to realize for the first time that everyone is staring. "What the fuck are you all looking at?"

Everyone quickly goes back to what they were doing before the fight broke out, fear of Jax's anger clearly winning out over their curiosity about what just happened.

Jax starts to stomp away, bloody footprints marking his path. I dodge around Patrick, even as he tries to stop me, and catch up to Jax just before he reaches the front door. "Where are you going?" I reach for his shoulder, his muscles tensing under my touch as he pauses with his back still to me.

"I'm getting the fuck out of here. Don't act like you give a shit." I'm so taken back by his sharp words that my head snaps back. I don't take my hand off his shoulder, I grip it tighter. Neither of us moves for a long moment. I've gotten so used to keeping Jax at a distance, but this time I know I'm the one that has to come to him. He stood up for me back there, despite the fact I would have much rather he fought with words than fists.

I take a deep breath and walk around so that I'm facing Jax from the front. "You can't leave like this. Let me help you clean yourself up, at least."

Even though Kareem took far more blows to the face, Jax still has a cut bleeding above his eye, forcing him to squint as he looks at me. There's a little cut by his lip too, but that one isn't nearly as bad. I can't imagine what he must look like under his shirt after Kareem got that kick in though. Surely he's bruised. Fuck, I hope he didn't crack a rib.

Even though Jax hasn't actually agreed, he stays silent as I take his hand to start leading him back the other way, towards the upstairs bathroom. I know there's a first aid kit up there because I had to help Salma bandage her finger earlier after she accidentally cut herself while chopping up limes. Jax's feet fall in heavy thuds as I pull him along with me, closing the bathroom door behind us before turning to rummage in the cabinet for the first aid kit.

I set the kit out on the counter of the bathroom sink, fumbling around until I find antiseptic wipes and bandages. It'll have to do. I would ask him to let me take him to the hospital to get cleaned up if I thought there was even the slightest chance he'd go, but even without asking I know there's no way he'll do it. He's putting up with me fretting over him, but his demeanor is like this is no big deal. Hell, for him maybe it's not. I can only imagine how many fights he's gotten into over the years. I know of at least one other time for sure—when Patrick gave him that black eye last year after Jax exposed me in the middle of our history project.

"You shouldn't have stepped in like that," I tell him softly as drag an antiseptic wipe across his bloody eyebrow. He winces, grabbing me by the wrist to pull my hand away from his face. "I'm sorry, I'm sure it stings but we really need to clean this."

He makes a grunting sound low in his throat that sounds like disagreement, but he lets go of my wrist and lets me continue. For a couple of minutes, I work in silence. The only sound between us the occasional groan as the antiseptic stings his cut. The cut by his mouth, on the other hand, is much easier to deal with. I went through about ten wipes on the cut above his eye, but this one takes just two. He huffs out a puff of breath just as I'm leaning closer to make sure I got it good enough. His breath

148

skates over my skin, sending goosebumps up my arms.

This was all business two seconds ago, but now I catch myself leaning closer as I toss away the last of the wipes. Jax eyes me warily, but the second my eyes dip to glance at his mouth, his hands go to my waist. This time, there's no question that I'm the one that closes the distance, my mouth finding his carefully as I worry in the back of my mind about hurting him.

Apparently, he doesn't share the same concern. He dives in with everything he's got, just the same as he always does. His lips parting as his tongue breaches my mouth, reminding me that when he kisses me, there's no real room for thinking about anything else. My mind turns to pure mush as he devours me right there in the middle of the bathroom. For a moment, there's pure magic between us.

Then, I try to shift even closer to him and he pulls away with a wince. It takes my hazy brain a second to remember he just got kicked right in the abdomen where I'm leaning into him. I jump back, my hip bumping the countertop painfully as I put as much space between us as I can.

God, the two of us really can't be left alone in any kind of enclosed space together. I study Jax's face as he stares back at me.

It's really unfair how goddamn sexy he is. He's been keeping the stubble along his jaw, which I love despite the slight rash I can already feel around my mouth. Fucking worth it. I'm really thinking about jumping at him again when his body goes defensive out of nowhere. His shoulders stiffen as his back goes ramrod straight. He wipes the back of his hand across his mouth and heads for the door as I stand there gaping at him.

It's only when he's opening the door that I manage to find words to throw at his back. "Stop fucking walking away from me before I'm finished."

14

Jax was halfway out the door, but my words stop him. He slowly backs himself back into the bathroom, calmly closing the door again. I can feel my heart racing in my chest, anxiety creeping in as I have no idea what's about to come. I'm not even remotely ready for him.

He storms back to me, my legs quivering when I see the heat in his eyes. I barely manage to keep up with what's happening as he grips my thighs to lift me up onto the bathroom counter, his hands pushing my shoulders until my back is leaning against the mirror on the wall. I can feel the cool glass through my thin shirt. He stands between my thighs, pushing them as far apart as they can comfortably go in my tight jeans, as he leans over me to reach my mouth. His hands run over every inch of me as he kisses me with a desperation that wasn't there before.

His lips slide over across my jaw and down my neck, stopping to suck the sensitive skin of my shoulder where my shirt doesn't cover. A low moan escapes me as I let my head fall back, eyes blinking up at the ceiling as he runs his hands over the inside seam of my jeans. I nearly buck myself right off the counter in surprise when one of his hands goes *all the way up*.

I tilt my head back down to look at him as his mouth leaves my shoulder, just in time to watch him working open the button on my jeans. I blink. It takes a second before it kicks in that this is a very, very bad idea.

"Woah. Wait." I reach a hand out to stop him.

It's like flipping a switch again. He releases me, jerking away and pacing across the bathroom to face the tiled shower wall. He laces his hands behind his neck as he bounces agitatedly on the balls of his feet.

"Why the fuck do you melt for everyone but me?" He turns to face me with fiery eyes, staying in his same spot. It's a big bathroom and he's put several feet between us. I open my mouth to protest—I don't *melt for everyone*—but he's not done. "I made shit happen for you when those guys were only chasing you around like desperate puppies. What the fuck did they do for you that I didn't? Ace, Smith, Patrick, tell me which one of them wasn't a dick to you when it suited them? And then what? They whisper sweet nothings in your ear and suddenly you forgot all about it?"

"That's not fair," I whisper.

"Isn't it?" I can't rise to meet the challenge in his eyes. *Because, yeah, he's sort of right.* "If I hadn't treated you like shit when you first got here, it would have been you that turned up dead instead of Kathryn. Hate me all you want, but the target I put on your fucking back was the only thing that kept you safe."

I hate myself for it a little bit, but I look away. There's too much emotion in his eyes, the kind of thing I've only ever seen in passing on Jax's face. Now, though, he's gutted by it. Anguish in his voice as finally I get the answers I haven't dared ask for.

I don't even have to question if it's true. The way he spits the words at me like he never planned to say them—no one can fake that. And he's absolutely right.

Everyone was hesitant with me because Jax deemed me unacceptable. If he hadn't, and the path had been paved for Kathryn to try to sink her claws into me, and by some weird twist of events I had actually let myself be dragged into her inner circle... It would no doubt have been me Cece focused her rage on for taking her place, instead of at Kathryn for wanting to replace her in the first place.

I could have been dead.

The silence is so heavy between us but I don't know how to break it. A "thank you" doesn't exactly seem appropriate at a moment like this. I guess he gets tired of waiting to see if I'm going to respond, because he shakes his head in disgust and starts for the door again. I slide off the bathroom counter, following him even though I have no idea what the hell to do. When he glances back at me while he's opening the door, his expression fucking breaks me. He looks disappointed—and dammit even though it makes no sense, I don't want to disappoint him.

"Wait." It's like some other force takes control of me as I gently push him out of the way of the door and close it again. Before, we only closed it, but this time I reach behind me and push the lock. The sound makes Jax's eyebrows furrow, and then he winces as the motion agitates the cut by his eye.

He watches me carefully as I walk back over in front of the sink. Our eyes stay steady on each other, never breaking eye contact even as the snap of me unbuttoning my jeans seems to echo louder than it should in this oversized bathroom. I push my jeans down my legs, eyes still on his. I can tell he's fighting not to look as I kick one leg out and then the other to work them all the way off. Pants now off, I put my palms behind me on the counter and lift myself up, putting myself back in the position I was in before I hit the brakes.

When Jax doesn't move right away, I start, "I told myself I wouldn't beg but—" I don't even have to finish the sentence.

He grabs desperately at the hem of my shirt, pulling it over my head and throwing it behind him as he drinks me in. I can feel nerves try to fight their way into my stomach, a self-consciousness warring within me about showing myself to someone in a bright room like this. I can feel myself tensing up, and apparently he can, too.

"Relax," he murmurs as he hooks one finger around the crotch of my panties.

Telling someone to relax while touching them intimately for the first time is not that fucking effective—but then he slides that one finger across my crease and I'm not thinking about anything anymore but how fucking good it feels to have Jax Woods touching me. It's like a goddamn art form this guy possesses as he teases me with just that one finger, touching me in a way no one else ever has. I grind against him as he teases me, closing my eyes as I try to cling to some semblance of control.

It's no use. Jax knows exactly what he's doing and it's not long before he's sending me over the edge into orgasmic euphoria. All with just that one goddamn finger.

I whimper as he pulls away from me, my cheeks reddening as the involuntary sound escapes me. As Jax starts to undress himself, I know that all the second-guessing is over and done with. I want this so fucking bad that I'm vibrating for him, my whole body humming with the need to take this so much farther than it's already gone. He sheaths himself with a condom as he steps back in between my legs, my eyes drinking him in. He's pure perfection. Still an asshole, but an asshole with the kind of body wet dreams are made of.

My hands reach out for him, pulling him closer so my fingers can tangle in his hair. His hands somehow manage to lift me up enough to slide my panties down my thighs. He has to pull away for a moment to take them the rest of the way off, but then he's right back against me, my bra the only thing between us now. And his fingers make quick work of that, too, reaching behind me to deftly strip me of my last piece of clothing.

There's nothing but skin on skin left. He blows out a long breath as he takes a good look at me, his eyes lingering on my bare breasts for a long moment before he looks up at my face again. "You're not—" he stops short. "Have you slept with them?" I'm assuming he means any of his friends. I shake my head no. "But you've done this before?"

"Yeah." I press a hand to his chest when he starts to lean in again. "But not, uh, a lot."

There's a spark of pleasure in his eyes as I divulge my lack of experience. *He likes that.* His hands skate up over my thighs, my hips, my stomach, and then come to rest with his fingers just barely brushing the edges of my breasts. I squirm, the feel of his hands so good but so not enough. He smirks, knowing exactly what he's doing. When he finally indulges me by brushing his thumbs over my nipples, my whole body arches up against him, his rock hard dick sliding against the sensitive skin between my legs. This is as close as two people can get to sex without actually having sex.

He doesn't move right away, and a sudden wave of fear crashes over me that he's going to stop things right here. Just turn and walk away and leave me here like this, needy and not fully satisfied. It would be one hell of a cruel joke to play.

"If you don't relax, there's no way I can fuck you without seriously hurting you. You're too nervous, I could barely get a finger inside of you." He's not even trying to be sexy, his voice is matter-of-fact, but damn if the words don't make me whimper anyway. I could probably get off just from hearing him talk about fucking me—and I can't even imagine how much easier that would be if it was actually dirty talk. I'm the most dangerous kind of spark right now, ready to go completely up in flames at any moment. "I need to know you're listening. Nod or something." He smirks like a guy who knows exactly how gone I am.

"I don't care. Please, Jax." I reach down between us, fully prepared to do all the heavy lifting myself if that's what it fucking takes. I can't wait another second. Every minute I've spent with Jax since I got here has been foreplay. And a whole year's worth of foreplay does not a help a girl with being patient.

He grabs my wrist before I've done much else than brush the head of his dick, but he still sucks in a sharp breath. "If you put that hand on me right now, neither one of us is going to be able to get what we both really want right now."

I nod, my eyes probably as wide as saucers as I let

the weight of his words sink in. It's not just me. He's dancing too close to the edge, too. We're too good together. Too hot. Too impatient. Too everything. I close my eyes as Jax plants one hand on my hip and then within seconds, I can feel him lining himself up, preparing to give me exactly what I asked for. *Begged for, really.* Just like he said I would.

He wasn't joking when he warned me it would hurt. I cry out as he enters me for the first time, the pain not much better than when I lost my virginity. He pauses, all of his muscles tightening from the effort it takes for him to hold still for me.

"Keep going," I tell him in a tight voice.

"Not until you fucking *relax.*" He moves just enough to give him access to something he's never done before. He kisses me softly. "I'm glad you came home," he whispers against my lips.

Whatever eternal resistance had still been holding out seems to give way with those words. I couldn't figure out why he thought I wasn't relaxed before, but I can feel it now as my body opens up to him, letting him ease the rest of the way into me. The pain is gone, replaced instead with blinding pleasure as he finally starts to actually fuck me.

He moves slower than I anticipated, slowly building up speed as he alternates kissing me and staring down at my body as he runs his hands over it. It's like he can't get enough of touching me. God, I can't get enough of it either.

I try move my body in time with his, but I'm a

complete mess. It isn't long before I'm coming undone all over again, my fingernails digging into his back as I hold on for dear fucking life. He slows slightly, letting me ride out the wave of pleasure without overwhelming me. My body quivers with aftershocks as he leans his cheek against mine.

"Tell me you like me," he mutters in my ear.

"What?" I'm not even sure how he can form a coherent sentence right now, and I'm sure as hell not sure how his brain is functioning enough to even think about something that major at this exact second.

"Tell me," he demands again, his hand snaking up into my hair and forcing my head back so that I'm looking into his eyes. I do love it when he yanks my hair, though it's a secret I have every intention of taking to my grave.

I don't want to say it. It feels too big. Too big for this bathroom. But he's gone still and I know he's just stubborn enough to stop if he doesn't get what he wants. I blink hard and force myself to turn the words over in my head. They're not untrue—but am I really ready to say them? Insecurity flashes through his eyes, and the second I see it I know there's no use holding back. We've already made things messy.

"I like you, Jax Woods."

Those are the magic words. He wastes no time driving into me again, his mouth fusing to mine as he finishes with jerky movements, kissing me until he has to stop as he groans out my name and stills. I barely even hear it over the sound of my own panting. I'm fucking spent. Everything I had I've handed right over to him, letting him drain me both physically and emotionally.

He's quiet as he helps me up, dressing himself before he starts handing me my clothes back one by one. Bra. Shirt. Pants. Uh…

"You forgot something," I point out, holding out my hand.

"I don't think I did, no." But he grins, so I know he knows exactly what I mean. *Fucking hell—Jax Woods wants to keep my panties.* Fuck it. I look pointedly at him as I tug my jeans on sans underwear. His grin widens.

When we're both dressed—and as overall collected as we're probably gonna get right now—Jax reaches around me to open the bathroom door, wrapping an arm around my waist from behind as we leave the room together. His hand snakes up the front of my shirt. It's not the easiest position for walking, but I'm not complaining, the feel of his hand splayed across my bare stomach helping me to reground myself.

The house is much quieter now than when we first disappeared into the bathroom. We pick our way quietly down the hall, but about halfway to the staircase we somehow manage to trip together, both of us ending up sprawled in the floor, me half on top of Jax from where he made sure to help break my fall. I laugh so hard I snort, and then Jax is laughing too and it's the most genuine, sweet thing I think I've ever heard. This is nothing like the cruel laugh I'm used to from him.

"Well this is fucking cozy." We both fall silent as Patrick comes to hover over us. He breathes in deeply, probably trying to tamp down the jealousy he knows I hate. He really has been working on it, and it shows. His narrowed eyes start to return to normal. He offers me a hand up, which I gladly take.

Jax gets up, too, but I almost wish he hadn't when he opens that fucking mouth of his. "Not nearly as cozy as it would have been if you'd walked in on us five minutes ago." He smirks at Patrick, glee flashing in his eyes as Patrick goes right back to being agitated. "Good news for you, though, isn't it? I told you all from the beginning she was off-limits until I had her first, but now the rest of you can consider it a fair game."

"A fair *game*? Really?" I back away from both of them, throwing my hands up for them to stay back when they both try to step towards me at the same time.

Jax's smirk falls as his mouth twists into a deep frown. "I didn't mean it like that." But how the hell does he expect me to believe that now? While he's busy gloating about having me first? No wonder he was so goddamned pleased with my lack of experience. He wanted to make sure he was fucking *winning* something by fucking me before his friends did.

How could I be so blind? Of course that's something he would do. He's Jax Woods. He doesn't give a shit about anyone but himself. And the guys, who spent all summer trying to convince me differently, were just fooling themselves.

Despite me waving at him to stay back, Jax closes the distance between us and lowers his voice. "Don't ruin what we just did." My mouth falls open.

"Are you kidding me? You think *I'm* the one ruining it? Take a look in a goddamn mirror." I push him away from me. I can't even stand to look at him right now. I force my feet to move toward the stairs. I don't want to look at either of them. I just want to go home.

15

I wring my hands nervously together as I wait for someone to answer the front door. I didn't like the way we left things last night, so I'm swallowing my pride and coming to fix it. Except, no one has answered the door yet and I've already rung the doorbell three times like a crazy person. I think it's time to accept that either no one's home or he just plain doesn't want to see me.

I take a few steps back toward my SUV before I hear the door open. I turn back, sagging with relief when Neema Dupont greets me with a wide smile. I retrace my steps back to the front door.

"Sorry, sweetie. There's a very lively debate about the merits of artificial intelligence going on in the living room. I almost didn't hear the door." Only in a headmaster's house would I ever expect to hear those words strung together like that. How many other families were sitting around debating artificial intelligence on a Saturday night?

I follow Neema into the house, and almost right away I hear what she was talking about. *Lively* debate is right. They're basically yelling at each other, and when we turn the corner into the living room, I see they're also standing toe-to-toe.

I've officially never seen anything like this. Neema calmly takes a seat on the couch as I hover by the doorway. It takes a second for Headmaster Dupont and Patrick to even realize I've joined them. When they do, their debate dies off. The headmaster offers me a warm smile, but Patrick glances away, avoiding looking at me. I'm sure he's mad at me for walking out on him last night, but I'm mad at him for making me feel like I had to. We need to hash it out, the way I hashed things out with Ace. Maybe then Patrick and I can move forward as easily as Ace and I have since then.

"Patrick." A wave of nerves suddenly hits me as I realize how horrifyingly embarrassing it's going to be if he denies me in front of his parents. "Will you take a drive with me?"

Neema clasps her hands in front of her chest. "Oh, Patty. Of course you should go. The two of you can go up to Churchill Point again." He covers his mouth with his hand as he turns away in embarrassment. If he's embarrassed about telling his mom we've gone up to Churchill Point together, he shouldn't be. I actually think it's cute. Gotta respect a guy that respects his mama enough to talk to her about his dating life.

After a moment, he makes himself face me. "You want me to drive?" he asks.

I shrug. "Sure." He knows the roads a lot better than I do. And I'm *pretty sure* he would never abandon me on the side of the road or anything.

He grabs his keys while I make small talk with his parents. They're really great people, and a part of me can't help but wonder if they'd be this nice to me if they knew their son wasn't the only boy I'm dating. Patrick might talk to his mom about dating me, but I'd be willing to bet all of Lexington Estate that he hasn't given her all the sordid details of our arrangement. His father on the other hand, I study him closely looking for any sign that he's picked anything up from the gossip mill at school. He certainly doesn't seem like he's keeping secret judgements to himself.

I tell them goodbye when Patrick returns, and we walk out together to his car. He doesn't take my hand, but he walks closely enough that our shoulders brush. I can smell his familiar woodsy cologne and as he opens the passenger side door for me, I pause to close my eyes and just breathe him in.

I only open them again when I feel a gentle touch caress my cheek. "It's really hard to be mad at you," Patrick says as he cups my face in both hands.

"That makes sense considering I'm the one that should be mad." He frowns but doesn't stop stroking his thumbs across my cheeks in soothing circles. "You keep letting your jealousy get the better of you. You shouldn't have agreed to date me like this if you couldn't actually handle it, Patrick."

"What I agreed to and what we're doing turned out to be two different things." He snorts. He starts ticking names off on his fingers. "There was Smith. And then surprise! There was Ace. And now there's Jax, despite the fact that you denied all summer that it would ever happen. There's always someone else. Every time I think I've gotten used to how it is, you're fucking someone else."

"That isn't fair." My voice shakes.

"No, that's right. Apparently, you're only actually fucking Woods."

There's so much venom in his voice and I can barely stomach it. I get what he's saying, I really do. We're in a relationship, we should talk about things, I shouldn't just be springing other people on him with no warning. But then that's something we should talk about, it shouldn't be an excuse for him to talk down to me like this. I get that he's used to being the king of the world everywhere else, but I only want a relationship where I get to feel like an equal. And that's something Patrick has struggled with ever since I got here.

"Maybe we shouldn't do this," I tell him, pulling out of his grasp and taking a step away from the car. I'm not going to drive out to what's supposed to be one of the most romantic spots in the whole city if all we're going to do is fight once we get there.

His eyes go wide with alarm. "Seriously. That's it, you're just done?"

"What? No!" I shake my head profusely. "I meant maybe we shouldn't go driving across town together when we're already fighting before we've even made it into the car."

"Oh." His posture relaxes as he swings the car door back and forth with one hand. "Look, I don't want this to be how things are. I don't want to be the boyfriend you fight with. I just want to be able to be prepared for what's going on, instead of always feeling like I'm being fucking blindsided."

"I think that's completely fair," I tell him, closing the distance between us again. "And I'm sorry that's not how it's been."

"Okay, so let's go for that drive, then."

Everything feels a little lighter now that we've acknowledged the elephant in the room. Patrick asks me about my classes, and I indulge him the way I would no one else—by telling him what's actually going on in my classes. Unlike other guys, I know he's not asking a generic question when he asks about school. He actually gives a shit. One of the best things about Patrick is how easy he is to talk to just because we're intellectual equals. I'm not sure how many other guys there are in the world that would care what I wrote my last English essay about.

Plus, we get to talk about Yearbook, which we

actually have together. I haven't done much more than take some club photos, but Patrick glows a little when he talks about the yearbook. It makes sense considering he's the editor.

"It's fun having two classes with you. That was a nice surprise," I muse since we're discussing classes. A weird silence descends. I glance over at Patrick to find him chewing his bottom lip. "What?"

"I might have manipulated your schedule a bit."

"Oh." I blink, processing that. He looks nervous as hell, but I quickly decide I'm not that bothered by it. "It's fine," I tell him.

"Really?"

"You had access to change my schedule and still left me in classes where I'm alone with Smith in one and Ace in another. You could've done a lot worse, but you didn't. So yeah, I'm not mad. I am curious, though. Was I not in Yearbook originally? I did think it was weird that I got put in a class you're supposed to have to fill out an application for."

Patrick wrinkles his nose. "They put you in theatre. But that seemed like..." He trails off.

"It would have been like they were giving me Cece's slot. Yeah, that's in seriously poor taste. Who the hell does the schedules?"

"The front office does most of the work, but Dr. Peterson has a say, too. Usually he would never let something like that slide." He shrugs casually as if it's not that big a deal, but something about that strikes me funny. The headmaster might not always know what's going around the school, but Dr. Peterson should. I wonder if trying to stick me into Cece's theatre spot was some weird power trip. A way to punish me for all the times I found excuses not to meet with him when he tried to schedule counseling sessions with me.

Patrick pulls into our spot at Churchill Point. It's always the same spot we come to, the same as the first time. This spot has the best view of the city. We don't have a blanket with us this time, so we sit on the grass side by side, me leaning into him as we look out over the city.

I sneak glances over at Patrick until finally I just drop the pretense and turn to look at him full-on. The whole city is laid out before us, but the only thing I want to look at is him.

I still think he's every bit as beautiful as the first time I saw him. When he was insulting my intelligence and Sadie was accusing him of spreading STDs—but I try not to think about those particular details. Instead, I think about seeing his honey-colored eyes for the first time and seeing that panty-melting smile of his. At the time, I never would have imagined the two of us would end up here.

"You could have anyone you wanted. Why me?"

He reaches out to take my hand, lacing his fingers through mine as his eyes study me. "How could it have been anyone else?"

He leans in to kiss me and I kiss him back, but there's something unfamiliar about the way he's kissing me. Sloppy and desperate in all the wrong kind of ways. Slowly, he starts to move over me, leaving me no choice but to lay back against the grass as he climbs over top of me. I try to stop the uneasy feeling in my stomach. I love kissing Patrick. Love the way he's usually so precise in every motion. So very him.

But this? This feels like I'm kissing someone else entirely.

I turn my head to the side, breaking the confusing kiss. "What's wrong?"

"Nothing's wrong," he mumbles.

It's a bullshit answer and I know it. Clearly something is wrong, because I don't recognize him as he pushes my sweatshirt up my midsection and starts tugging at the waistband of my leggings. There's nothing sexy or practiced about it. He's being erratic and stiff, and there's nothing special about him trying to unceremoniously strip me down in the middle of a public park in broad daylight.

I push his shoulder, making him roll off of me. He lets his head drop back against the ground as he lets out a frustrated groan.

"Why are you trying to do this right now?" This isn't how I imagined being intimate with Patrick for the first time. For being such a ladies man, he's sure not living up to expectations at the moment. He's experienced. I know he is. There's no way he thinks this is really acceptable for anything more than a quickie between two people who have no intention of being serious together. And that's not even remotely how I view our relationship. I like to imagine he doesn't either but after this—shit, I don't know.

"Because I love you," he spits out with an irritated tone that doesn't match what he's claiming.

A heavy weight settles in my chest. "How can you say that right now?" He isn't even looking *at* me, but *through* me. "Those words mean something to me. Saying them right now, when things are obviously getting really weird between us, it's like you're turning them into a joke."

"Yeah, I get it." He climbs to his feet, apparently just so he can stare down angrily at me, since he doesn't go far. "I'm not good enough to be a priority. I'm not good enough to fuck. And now I'm not good enough to say I love you."

"That isn't what I said and you know it."

Fuck this. I climb to my feet and walk away from him, not even bothering to see if he follows. If he doesn't, I'll fucking walk home if I have to. Right now I'm so mad my adrenaline is egging me on, telling me I could run a marathon if I needed to.

"Where are you going?" Patrick calls after me.

"Back to the car. I knew this was a mistake before we even got in the car and I should have listened to my gut." He says something else but I hum under my breath to tune him out. Because I swear, if he doesn't stop I'm going to end up on TV for pushing his ass off the ledge of Churchill Point, and that's not really the family legacy I was hoping to help leave.

I climb into the unlocked car, arms crossed, and eyes trained out the passenger side window. I don't look at him or speak as he joins me. He just sits there as if he's waiting for me to break and speak first.

"I think—" he starts to say, but I cut him off.

"I want to go home."

"But—"

"Patrick. If you don't start this car and drive me the fuck back, this isn't going to be fixable anymore. Give me some fucking space, so that I can figure out how the hell I'm supposed to face you again after what you just pulled back there." I'm so angry I can practically taste my own bitterness on my tongue.

Patrick does start the car and turn toward home, but a few minutes into the drive he makes a frustrated noise deep in his throat. "I don't understand why you're so mad. If you didn't want to mess around all you had to do was say that." I laugh humorlessly, the sound so pathetic as it echoes through the car.

"I would have been thrilled to fool around with you. If only it had been about me and you—the way it should have been—instead of about you being caught up in what happened between me and Jax."

He doesn't try to talk to me again after that. The rest of the drive is silent.

16

Why am I here?

The detention center looms ominously in front of me as a guard checks my ID and waves me through the gate. I park in the designated lot and slowly make my way to the front doors. It's the sound of crying that hits me first. The front lobby is like a haven for wailing mothers and I'm relieved Cece's mother isn't among them. If she'd been here, this plan would have gone straight to hell.

I'm following Sadie's instructions down to the letter. *Show up for the earliest possible visitation. You're more likely to find someone working that's new and less sure of the rules. Dress young. Cry if you have to.* I'm lucky that even though she didn't agree with what I was doing, she was willing to help me. Apparently, Sadie's had a friend or two in juvie over the years, so she knew all about how to get around the family-only rules.

This place is nothing like how I've heard juvie described in Nikon Park. I imagine the demographics around here have something to do with that. Even though the detention center's not in Patience, it's close enough that pretty much everyone here has to be from nearby—and there's nothing but rich people for miles, basically.

I go through security, trying not to cringe at the gruff way the guards speak to me as they direct me how they want me to pass through. It's weird feeling like I'm being treated like a criminal just by association.

As I pass into the area where visitors are actually checking in, I see two lines. I study the two women working closely before choosing my line. I go with the younger of the two, the one who's smile is a little too bright and definitely forced. She looks like she's a little slower, too, which I'm guessing is because the other woman is more experienced.

"Step on up," she waves me closer when it's my turn. "ID, please." She taps a paper on the countertop. "And fill this out for me."

I hand my ID over and she starts doing something on her computer as I fill out the form. It's just basic stuff about who I am and who I'm visiting. I breeze through it quickly and hand it to her. She thanks me quietly and continues doing whatever it is she's doing on her computer. After a minute, she looks up.

The woman frowns at me as she looks from me

to my ID. "What's your relationship to the person you're visiting?" It's on the paper, but I'm sure she's wondering if she's going to catch me in a lie.

"Stepsister," I answer with my best poker face.

She looks down at her computer screen, squinting hard like she's afraid she missed something, then back to me. "Your name isn't on her family visitation sheet."

I make a big show out of widening my eyes and quivering my bottom lip. "Our parents were married when we were younger, but they're divorced now. But we've always kept in touch. She really didn't put me on there?" I sniffle as if fighting back tears.

The lady falters, clearly not prepared to handle the threat of a crying teenager on top of all these crying mothers. "I'm sure it was just a mistake, sweetie," she whispers. She hands me back my ID and my stomach sinks as I wait for her to tell me I have to leave.

For a second, she doesn't say anything and I tell myself just to turn and go. This was a stupid idea. Then, slowly, she slides a key across the counter to me. She looks me straight in the eyes, her eyes wide like she's begging me not to do anything to draw attention to us. She's breaking the rules for me. Big time.

"You'll leave any personal items in the lockers to the right and you can retrieve them again after your visit," she says casually, the same as I'm sure she'd explain this to anyone else. But her smile is tight like

175

she's still worried someone's going to notice what's happening somehow.

I smile and mouth *thank you* as I take the key from her, fighting back a grin when she shoots me a conspiratorial wink. *I can't believe I actually pulled that off.*

I go through the rest of the steps, locking my things in a locker and going through another round of security before I'm taken to a big open room with small, cafeteria-style tables. A guard directs all of us to have a seat as we wait for the girls to be brought out. I still feel major imposter syndrome, like someone is gonna turn and point out that I don't belong at any minute. This is pretty major rule-breaking I'm doing right now to be here. I only hope it's freaking worth it.

I tap my fingers nervously on the table as I wait. I'm not waiting for long before a buzzer sounds and a metal door clicks open on the far side of the room. A line of girls escorted by several guards enter. The guards watch like hawks as the girls each go to greet their families. Cece pauses just inside the door, eyes scanning the room before they land on me. Surprise causes her eyebrows to arch. She didn't know I was coming, and this whole plan could fall apart right here if she protests, but she purses her lips and starts towards me without a word to any of the guards.

I never considered what it would actually feel like to have her walking towards me, to make the conscious choice to sit down with a killer. My hands are clammy as I rest my palms against the table while she joins me. Cece watches me carefully, her lips slightly turned up in the corners. It's not quite a smile, but it's close enough to be unnerving.

"That's a great color on you," she gushes, leaning her elbows on the table. I look down, puzzled by her compliment, at my plain black shirt. "Not the clothes, silly. The lip gloss. Kathryn used to wear a great color just like that." Her expression falters. "But then she started wearing one of those long-lasting lip stains so she could get away with fooling around with Harrington without anyone knowing. The lip stain doesn't smear, but it's not nearly as pretty."

I can't believe I'm sitting in front of her in Juvie and all she wants to talk about is my choice of makeup. At least she isn't belligerent like the last time I saw her. That's something, I guess.

"Thanks, Cece." Seeing her like this, it's hard not revert back to feeling sorry for her. I still vividly remember the shitty way Kathryn treated her, and even though that wasn't an excuse to kill her, it isn't hard to see how Cece finally managed to snap.

"So." Cece studies me with shrewd eyes. "You finally came looking for answers, did you?" She looks smug as she leans back, crossing her arms over herself with a smile tugging one corner of her lips up even higher.

I'm not quite ready to ask her about what Brock Forrester said. I choose a different tactic. "You'll never believe what the school tried to do." She raises an eyebrow. Where her face was once perfectly manicured, her eyebrows now are darker and fuller. I actually think she looks better this way. More natural. "They tried to put me in Theatre."

Her arms fall away as she shifts in the seat. I can see right away that the news has jarred her. I'm sure she thought she would be irreplaceable, and in a way she was. Everyone has said the theatre department is barely holding it together since her arrest. Apparently, Cece's family's money was stretching a long way to help them put on those big productions that Cece starred in, and now no one can see to figure out how to keep things running the way she did.

"But you don't care about theatre." She doesn't say it as an insult or like she's offended. She was glad when I arrived and had no intention of trying to undercut her position in the school's theatre program.

"Yeah, Patrick got me put in Yearbook instead."

Cece nods thoughtfully. "That makes much more sense. A good Patience queen should have her finger on the pulse. Yearbook is a good class for that. You see all the pictures of who's doing what with who. That's good information, make sure you use that."

I didn't come here for lessons on being popular—though, damn, I would never have even considered taking advantage of being in Yearbook like that. Say what you want about Cece, she clearly knew how to keep *her* finger on the pulse. I wonder how many times Kathryn used that to her own advantage? It was never any secret that Kathryn's special skills were treating people like shit and taking advantage of Cece.

"Cece, I actually came because—"

"No, wait! Let me guess!" she interrupts excitedly. It's almost starting to feel like she's running out the clock on our visit. "You want to know what Jax and I did in the bedroom?" She wiggles her eyebrows, but then her face falls. "You slept with him, didn't you?" With a sigh, she angles her body away as if she can't stand to look at me now. "Of course you did. You were the girl that left and now you're the girl that came back. He was so obsessed with you. Of course you slept with him. No one can resist Jax Woods."

"What do you mean obsessed with me?" Obsessed with being an asshole to me, maybe.

She waves her hand in the air meaninglessly until a guard warns her to quit playing around and she drops her hands back to her lap. "Y'know. Obsessed. Watching you every time you walked into a room. Asking people about you. Going all growly when *other people* asked about you."

"That's crazy," I say before I can think twice about my choice of words. It doesn't seem to faze Cece, though.

"But you slept with him. So part of you has to know it's true." She shrugs. "Either that or you're the worst masochist ever, I guess."

I didn't come here to talk about who I'm sleeping

with. And since this is making me super uncomfortable, I figure it's now or never. "Cece, Brock Forrester said something about you that's been bothering me. Brent Forrester's dad?"

"Oh, sweetie. I know exactly who Brock Forrester is." She gets a dreamy look in her eyes. "Kathryn was totally obsessed with him. She made me sleep with Brent just to get his dad's work schedule so she could *just so happen* to run into him at the country club. Did you know that?" She smiles, but it doesn't reach her eyes. "I don't recommend it. Brent throws a good party, but he's terrible in bed. I'm not sure he knows the difference between a clit and a taint." *Gross. And way more information than I ever wanted to hear about my classmate.*

"He seemed to think maybe you were a little bit sneaky or something. Like maybe you were fooling around with guys at the club and getting information you shouldn't have." She stares at me blankly, clearly far more interested in this direction of the conversation than she is about telling me about her former sex life.

"Is there a question in there, or are you accusing me of something?"

I quirk one eyebrow. "I'm not accusing you of anything," I tell her honestly. "It just seemed like Mr. Forrester thought you knew something that would mean something to me. That's all."

Cece pushes her hair behind her ear as she stares across the table wordlessly at me. She's had it cut several inches shorter since the last time I saw her—when she was arrested on Prom night. I can see where her roots are growing in from lack of bleaching too, but I try not to stare. Cece's already going to be punished for what she did to Kathryn. I don't need to add insult to injury by making her self-conscious. Especially not when I came here asking for information.

"I know a lot of things," she says quietly, glancing around like she's worried someone might eavesdrop. "But the one thing I know that you really ought to know—you're being played."

"What?"

"I wonder if he really underestimated you, or if he just got distracted having a tight, young body in front of him." She gives me a calculated perusal that makes me uncomfortable enough that I cross my arms over my chest.

"What the hell are you talking about?" I ask.

"Brock Forrester is trying to distract you. I'm sure he thought if he told you I knew something that you'd start creeping around looking for answers. He probably never imagined you'd have the balls to come straight to the source." She shakes her head and clicks her tongue. I'm starting to believe at least one thing Brock said. Cece was putting on an act. The way she's talking now? She's not ditzy or clueless, she's just throwing everyone for a loop. Just like she seems so proud of me for doing. "I'll admit, I was guilty of underestimating you, myself."

What she's saying is a lot to unpack. But why would Brock go through all that trouble just to send me on a wild goose-chase?

"What would he be trying to distract me from?"

"Haven't you realized it yet, Juliet? He wants what everyone wants—Hollis Lexington's treasure." She rolls her eyes as if the whole thing is overrated and she's tired of talking about it. "Most of them, they're using their kids to get to you, but Brock? His son's not the brightest or most interesting bulb in the pack. He probably figures it's easier just to do the dirty work himself."

Brock Forrester told me he didn't believe in the hype about Hollis' treasure. I repeat the words aloud to Cece. She laughs in disbelief as she looks down her nose at me.

"And you actually believed him?"

I try to remember exactly what Brock's words were that first night I met him. *"It's like our own personal urban legend. Nearly everyone in this damned town has tried their hand at Hollis' treasure hunt."* He said something else, too. *"Some people are more obsessed than others."*

I thought he was being cavalier because he genuinely didn't care, but was that an act? I've already seen for myself that I'm not great at judging the intentions of people around here. If I'd been better at it, I probably would have spent a hell of a lot less time being hurt over the past year. So, what if he wasn't being cavalier because he didn't care?

What if he was being cavalier because he did? What if he thought acting that way might cause me to slip up and say something I shouldn't?

There are too many *what ifs*. Like what if Cece is the one lying, and not Brock? I really have no way of knowing.

Except Cece has nothing to gain from lying, and it sounds like maybe Brock does.

"Are we done talking about you now?" Cece asks. "Because I've just been dying to tell someone how it's going in here."

"Sure, of course. Go ahead." I'm not so sure I want to know, but I'm not exactly sure I want to be rude to someone who literally killed another person. Besides, she's still human. Still capable of feeling lonely, and maybe I shouldn't, but I catch myself sympathizing with that a little bit.

Cece clasps her hands together in front of her face as her eyes light up. "I'm the fucking queen of this place." If she was being quiet and discreet before, she's the opposite now. Speaking up and reveling in the way it makes other people glance over at us. Based on the way her fellow detainees quickly look away, I don't think she's joking. She lowers her voice again. "I've done a lot of shit in here, Juliet, but it's not so different from the outside. If you make yourself indispensable, you can float to the top. And it's better here really, because there's no Kathryns or Juliets here to compete with." She glances at the girl at the table next to us. "Only

Jessicas and Ashleys with sad backstories and bad haircuts."

I don't even bother to point out that I grew up as a Jessica with a sad backstory—and I had more than my fair share of bad haircuts over the years. In different circumstances, it easily could have been me she was talking about.

"See this?" She turns her arm over to show me a long, thick, fresh scar running up the inside of her arm. "Patience girls use their words to hurt you and try to steal your crown. But here, these girls fight it out. I've got a few of these battle scars. But every time, I come out on top. Here, I'm the one being underestimated. They think Patience girls can't fight, but I grew up with older brothers. I can hold my own." She looks so proud as she tells me all of this, but it makes me feel sorry for her. She's in here because she was willing to hurt someone to be on top, and now she's here doing the same shit on a smaller scale.

"It sounds to me like being the queen isn't all it's cracked up to be."

Her eyes go wide with horror. "No, it is! Being queen isn't just *everything*, it's the *only thing*. Have you ever played Chess, Juliet?"

"I mean, a little bit over the years, but nothing serious. Why?" Where is she going with this?

She drags her finger across the table like she's drawing out a chess board. She points to a spot on the far side, closest to me. "The queen has all the power. She might be the last to get involved in things, but she's always the true center of the game." She traces a path forward to the invisible row on the front of my side of the imaginary board. "And then there are the pawns. Do you know what pawns get?"

I hate that this is sort of making sense so far. "What?"

"Pawns get killed."

She flattens her hand and smacks the table so hard I practically feel my bones rattle as I startle right out of my seat. As the guards start to head our way, she throws her head back and laughs.

"Visit's over," one of the guards tells me gruffly as Cece just keeps laughing. The sound of it is haunting, the kind of laugh someone gets when they're no longer in possession of anything resembling sanity. It's a symbol of just how far Cece has fallen.

The sound of that laugh follows me all the way out—out of the room, into the car, and all the way back to Patience.

17

After my bewildering visit to Cece, I go seeking out the one person I can always count on for easy comfort. Horses greet me at the pasture fence as I park my car up by the house, pulling over to the side of the garage like I was told. I slide out and go to meet the horses at the fence, cooing at them as I pet them down the length of their long faces. There's four of them, but three of them wander off when they realize I've got nothing to feed them. Only the littlest one stays, so I give her my full attention. And that's where Ace finds me still standing several minutes later.

"I should have known I'd find you out here. I'm starting to think you like the horses more than me." He wraps his arms around me from behind and I let my eyes close as I relax against him.

"Well, there is a lot of them and only one of you,"

I tease. He pinches my side, eliciting a giggle out of me.

"You're lucky I love you," he says, dropping a kiss on my shoulder. The words make me melt. "Let's get you inside, though. It's about to rain." I look up at the sky, noticing the dark clouds rolling in for the first time. That seems all too fitting.

We make it into the house just in time to miss the start of a downpour. Ace starts to lead me into the front living room, but he pauses on the threshold. "Hey," he greets someone. I peek around him to see a tall woman stretched across the couch, her head laying in a guy's lap.

The woman catches sight of me and bolts up. She smacks the guy on the chest. "Babe, look. Asher finally brought a girl home." She says it in a sing-song voice, obviously teasing him.

"Whit," Ace growls, his cheeks tinged pink.

She laughs and stands up, stretching out as my eyes go wide at the sight of her full height. She's definitely got to be related. She's nearly as tall as Ace is. I have to tilt my head up as she comes over to greet me, offering me her hand—also enormous.

"Hi," she says. "I'm Whitley. Asher's favorite sister."

"Only sister," he points out, shaking his head when she waves him off.

"What'd you do, Asher? Go and get a girlfriend and not tell us?" She reaches out and ruffles his hair. I start to get a weird feeling. Smith and Patrick's families both know about me more or less, but his sister seems genuinely surprised by my presence. Has he really not told them anything? I glance at him, waiting for him to answer. I think I'm as curious to hear his answer as Whitley is.

Ace is silent for an uncomfortably long moment before he says, "Just mind your own business, Whit." Okay, great. That's about the worst thing he could have said right now. I could understand not wanting his family to know maybe the exact details of our relationship, but refusing to answer outright is like next level bad. My heart feels like it's sinking down into the pit of my own stomach.

Whitley's eyes narrow. "I'm sorry, what's your name?" she asks, looking at me again as she ignores Ace's warning. I hadn't even realized I hadn't given it.

"Juliet," I tell her with a polite smile.

I regret it almost immediately when her eyes shoot to Ace, something not so happy flaring in them. "Is this a joke?" she asks him. "Dad's gonna freak out, Asher."

Great. This is getting better by the second. Not only is Ace not owning up to our relationship, but he's not owning up to our relationship because his dad isn't gonna approve. I've never had a parent blatantly not approve of me.

Ace looks over at me with an apology written all over his face, but it doesn't make me feel any better. "It's not personal, J." *It feels pretty damn personal.*

"It's because you're a Lexington," Whitley supplies, saying my last name with disdain. "Dad's convinced your grandfather was blackmailing him, and that his hidden treasure has something to do with it. He wants your so-called family treasure to stay buried, but you showing up here after all this time renewed everyone's interest in finding it."

None of that is *my* fault, I want to point out, but I stay silent. I don't want to get in the middle of it. I've barely made it in the front door and I'm basically being told that I'm not wanted here. I had no idea Ace's dad had issues with my family. He never mentioned it.

Something in the back of my mind waves flashing lights at me. He's never mentioned there being an issue between our families, but there was *something*. Last year, he was the one I asked about the family feud between the Lexingtons and the Harringtons. But if I'm remembering correctly, he got all weird and tense like he thought I was going to ask about something else. This is it. It has to be. If I'd been paying more attention, I might have realized earlier that there was an issue. But then all that shit went down between Ace and me where we didn't talk for months. So I'd forgotten all about it.

"I should go," I say quietly, flicking my eyes to Ace.

"Please don't. I want you here." He gives me big, sad puppy dog eyes.

I can see Whitley watching him, seeing the way

he's looking at me. She seems to soften back to how she was when we first walked in. "Asher's right," she says. "You should stay. Dad's not here anyway, and honestly the whole thing is stupid." Beside me, Ace breathes out a soft sigh of relief. He seems a little surprised that she's siding with him.

"If it helps, I'm pretty sure someone would have found whatever the treasure is by now if Hollis had really left anything behind. It's not like Lexington Estate is under lock and key." Just last week, one of Pearl's nurses called the cops because she saw someone prowling around outside when she was on her break. More and more, I'm really starting to believe that maybe Hollis really did only leave behind an unsolvable mystery.

"I'm sure you're right," Whitley nods, but I can see in her eyes that she's not actually convinced. In any case, the tension from before is gone.

Whitley introduces me to her husband and explains that they're just visiting to check out a couple horses Ace's dad is going to sell them. Ace's mentioned before that his sister lives down south on a farm of her own. We all talk for several minutes before Ace excuses us to be alone.

"I'm so fucking sorry about that," he murmurs as he tugs me through the house. Since his sister's in the informal living room, he pulls me into a more formal one at the back of the house. I look around, confused about the setup here. Ace notices and explains, "When Dad's got business, he directs people to come in through the back." He points out a door that leads directly outside. "Before my mom ditched us to start a new family in a new country," he makes a face, "She always complained about mud being tracked into the house. So, this was the solution and it's been this way ever since."

I hate to hear Ace talk about his mom, not that he does it often. I'm not sure how any woman could abandon their three kids and start a new family with someone else like they never existed. Then again, my mother tried to sell me to a man in the mob, so I know all about dysfunctional family life.

"Am I never gonna be able to meet your dad, Ace?" I've always thought of meeting people's families a normal part of dating. And even though there isn't much about my dating scenario that is normal, there's still a sense of tradition that I thought I would get to keep.

He runs a hand over his face. "I want you to meet my dad. Of course I do, J. I'm just… not quite sure how to broach the topic yet." He steps towards me, sliding his arms around my waist and kissing me softly. "But I will. I promise. And it'll be okay, my dad might have a lot of opinions about your family, but he's a good guy. He'll be able to look past it."

I have to believe he's right. He knows his dad better than I do.

"Now," Ace changes the subject, "I really, really don't want to talk about my family anymore."

His voice is huskier as his eyelids start to droop.

This isn't why I'm here, but dammit now it's all I can think about. I tilt my chin up so he can kiss me more fully, wanting that more than anything. He indulges me, going right from zero to sixty as he parts his lips, mine automatically following suit. And I'm not sure why this has become our new favorite habit, but all of a sudden he's pushing me back against the bookshelf lining the back wall. I loop my arms around his neck as he lifts me, my legs wrapping around him naturally.

I can feel the ridges on the spines of the books digging into my back but it doesn't stop me from moaning into Ace's mouth as I feel him hardening against me. The longer we kiss, the harder he gets, until I can practically feel his body pulsing towards mine, begging for this to go further. My body arches against him as it begs for the exact same thing.

Grudgingly, I break the kiss, knowing if I don't stop now I'm not going to be able to stop at all. He stops kissing me, but he doesn't let me go. Our kiss might have been hot, but just letting him hold me is something altogether different. It's sweet—even with his dick still pressed against me in the most suggestive possible way. Not that I'm complaining. There's nothing sexier than having that *concrete* evidence of how much he wants me. I'm just still not convinced we're ready. Admittedly, I still have my worries that he hasn't properly worked through what Celia did to him.

"I love you," I tell him softly, leaning in to kiss

only the corner of his mouth. I'm not looking to start either of us back up again.

"I love you, too, J."

He kisses me one more time—also on just the corner of the mouth—before setting me down. Then, he offers me a seat on the couch next to him. I lean into him as we sit facing the window overlooking more pastures. It's insane the size of this property. Their land could basically be its own little town.

When I'm ready, I tell him all about what happened with Cece. And then, because I have to fill in some gaps, I go back and tell him about all my interactions with Brock Forrester, too. When I'm finished, he grimaces as he seems to really choose his words carefully.

"As much as I hate to agree with Cece, I think Forrester fed you some serious bullshit. His kid used to talk so much shit when we were younger about finding your treasure. He had to have picked that up from somewhere. The rest of us, we didn't really talk openly about Hollis' whole treasure thing. It was something people mostly talked about just at home because everyone's parents were so obsessed. Even now, since you showed up, it's something people whisper about amongst themselves."

He squints for a second, looking off into the distance like he's trying to remember something. "I'm actually pretty sure he got the police called on him a few times in middle school for refusing to leave the property when Pearl caught him tres-passing."

"Ugh." I can't believe I got played.

Frustrated, I let my head fall against the back of the couch, twisting my neck sideways as I stare aimlessly towards the bookshelves. I have no idea how or why, but my eyes catch on a book and suddenly I can't shake this weird feeling. I stand up, cross the room, and take the book from the shelf without saying a word. I open the front cover and *there it is*.

It is not down on any map; true places never are.

"What are you doing?" Ace asks curiously, walking over to see what I'm looking at.

I close the book carefully, not wanting to draw any attention to what's on the inside. Considering he doesn't mention the inscription, I'm pretty sure he either doesn't know about it, or at least doesn't realize it means anything. I don't like keeping secrets, but the significance of this book feels like something I'm not ready to talk about with Ace. Not until I know what it actually means.

"Moby Dick?" He gives me a confused smile. "What? Are you a fan?"

"Yeah, actually. Would you mind if maybe I borrowed this?" I'm trying to sound casual, like it's no big deal.

He shrugs. "Sure, I don't see why not. It's my dad's, but I've never actually seen him read it, so I can't imagine he'll even notice it's gone."

"Thanks." I stand on my tiptoes so I can reach him for a kiss. "Hey, I probably need to get going. Will you walk me out now that the rain has stopped?"

I can hear my heart pounding in my ears as Ace walks me out to my car, pausing just long enough for me to say goodbye to his sister and brother-in-law before I go. We share one last kiss before I climb into the car, carefully setting Francis Van Doren's copy of Moby Dick on the seat beside me. Things just got very, very interesting.

18

I've barely put the car in park before I fling the door open, the book tucked under my arm as I dart from my driveway to Smith's house. I called him to tell him I was on my way over, though I didn't mention why, so the front door opens just as I'm reaching it.

"Woah." He puts his hands up to catch me as I nearly bowl him over. "What's going on?"

I take a deep breath and thrust the book out to him, watching his face as he turns it over in his hands. "Open it," I tell him. He looks at me curiously but does what I asked, eyes skimming over the inscription.

"Okay, what exactly has you in such a panic? Did you find something new in here?" He squints at the page like something new might appear right before his eyes. But I shake my head profusely as I point to the book.

"Smith. That's not the book you gave me." He

starts to shake his head like he doesn't get it, but then his mouth falls open as understanding finally hits him. *Now he gets it.* He grabs me by the hand and pulls me into the house with him. No one else is around he leads me upstairs into what I'm assuming is his bedroom. I look around, wanting to take it all in as I see his room for the first time. It's a little bit distracting from the matter at hand. More so because of how worked up I got not that long ago at Ace's. All kinds of inappropriately timed thoughts start running through my mind.

"Where did you get this?" Smith asks, bringing me back to why I'm actually here. He turns it over in his hands and checks out the inscription again.

"It belongs to Ace's dad." Smith jerks his head up to stare at me. "I didn't tell him anything. I don't even think he knew there was an inscription in there. I asked him if I could borrow it but I didn't explain why." I pause before telling him, "I am gonna have to tell him at some point though, Smith."

"I agree," he says. "Don't look so surprised. We're all on the same side, Jules."

I guess he's right. I shouldn't be so surprised that he's willing to turn this into a group thing. He's already proven he's far better at handling our relationship dynamic than the other guys. There's never any jealousy or sense of discomfort about it. Smith *likes* sharing me. Which is baffling and hot as hell all the same time somehow. I don't understand it—but I'm sure not about to question it either.

"Ace and his sister mentioned that their dad was maybe being blackmailed by Hollis? And that he thinks Hollis' treasure has something to do with that. Do you think he could be right? If Hollis gave Francis Van Doren this book, it's possible..."

"He could have been taunting him," Smith finishes for me with a grimace. "Yeah, that doesn't exactly bode well for anyone, does it? But we don't even know if that's true. There are a lot of theories, but obviously no one can prove anything without actually finding whatever Hollis hid."

I blow out a frustrated breath. Every time it seems like maybe we're onto something, we just turn up more questions. It's really just a never-ending puzzle and I can't help wondering if Hollis is laughing at us right now from beyond the grave. I let my eyes wander the room as I try to tamper down some of the disappointment I feel that this huge clue still doesn't actually lead to anything.

My eyes stop on a bong sitting on Smith's dresser. It's fancy and metallic, much nicer than anything anyone smoked out of in Nikon Park. Still, seeing the bong out in the open like this leaves me with a lot of questions. Like, what if pot wasn't the only thing he was doing? It was obvious when Sadie had a problem, but I know it doesn't always work like that. Some addicts function better than others.

"I stopped," Smith says, startling me out of my thoughts.

I look down at my feet for a second, a little

embarrassed to be caught staring like that. "You don't have to say that just for my sake. Just because I don't do it doesn't mean I'm judging you. It just made me wonder if the pot's the only thing. I've never seen you... but that doesn't mean..." I'm really struggling through finding the right words.

Smith grabs my hands and pulls me to him. "I'm not just saying it. I smoked a lot before you came because every day was so fucking boring. It was just a way to get through it with minimal participation. But nothing's been boring since you showed up, Juliet." He puts a finger under my chin, tilting my head up and kisses me. Soft, closed-mouth kisses that are more about reassurance than lust. He continues, "And yeah, the pot was the only thing. And some drinking occasionally, which you know, but only because I don't have to fight that same compulsion that Sadie and my mom have."

"I'm glad you don't." I could spend the rest of my life in Patience, but I know that I'll never forget the things I saw in Nikon Park. Addiction is hard and messy and it hurts everyone. I've been on the receiving end of that far more than my fair share of times.

I kiss Smith back the way he kissed me. Soft. Unassuming. But that's not nearly enough. I put a hand on his shoulder as I angle my head and kiss him again, running my tongue along his top lip as I silently ask him to kiss me back for real. He indulges me, opening his mouth to me for a real kiss.

I pull away just long enough to tug him towards his bed. For a split second he hesitates, but then he tumbles down onto the rumpled sheets with me, shoving his heavy comforter out of the way as he lays down facing me, his body half covering mine as we kiss languidly—like we've got all the time in the world together.

He leans on one arm while he keeps his other one free, his hand exploring the length of me over my clothes. He cups me through my bra, kneading that handful of flesh as my shoulders dig into the mattress, my chest straining out to meet his touch. We don't last long like that before Smith's climbing the rest of the way over me, kissing me harder as the neediness between us grows more desperate.

He abandons my mouth as he kisses his way down my neck, drawing little mewling sounds out of me as he runs his mouth over patches of overly sensitive skin. Wanting to push things further, I slide an arm in between our bodies.

My hand skates across the front of his jeans, tracing the length of him with my fingertips. His hips jerk slightly as he lets out a shuddering breath. I move my hand up, fingers dipping into the waistband of his jeans. He tenses, but when I don't move right away, his body relaxes back against mine.

I slowly start to slide my hand the rest of the way into his pants, lucky that his jeans are just loose enough to let me in. The tips of my fingers barely get a chance to make contact with his soft skin before he jerks away from me. He blinks down at me with confusion like he's not sure how things even got this far.

"Hey." He grabs my wrist and pulls my hand from his pants to stop me from venturing any further. "Let's not do that right now."

After all the time I've spent exploring blatant consent with Ace, I feel bad that the first word out of my mouth is, "No." Hastily, I add, "I'm ready now." I kiss him again.

"I'm not," he says with a hoarse voice and the shake of his head.

I drop my arms, letting them fall limp to either side of me on the bed. "Are you serious?" It's not like this is coming out of nowhere. Smith and I are good at stealing intimate moments. Kissing. Some over-the-clothes petting when we can get away with it. It's not like we've rushed into this. I've been with Smith the longest out of my guys. And we have good chemistry, so I know it's not that, either. "What's the problem?" My voice wobbles.

"Uh, this just isn't how I pictured it." He looks away from me as he rolls off of me, pushing himself off the bed and crossing the room so he's as far away from me as physically possible without actually leaving the room.

I look around, trying to figure out what the hell he means. It's not like we're hanging in a sketchy back alley or something. This is his bedroom. We have privacy. We have time. We have feelings. To me, that's exactly how I've pictured it. I don't know why he would picture it any other way. "I don't understand what the problem is," I push, frustration seeping into my voice.

"We don't have to talk about that right now," he says. "Let's do something else. We could do that ice cream place you like." Any other time, I'd jump right on that suggestion, but it's obviously a ploy to avoid actually talking. To me, that's a big no-no. Whatever's going on, I'd rather have it out in the open. Better to address it now than to let it simmer until it's a bigger problem than it needed to be in the first place.

I scoot closer to the edge of the bed and cross my arms below my chest. Smith's eyes flicker down to where my arms are pushing my breasts up like an offering. He mumbles what sounds like a curse as he tears his eyes away. *I don't get it. He's obviously turned on by me.*

"You're being stupid," I tell him with a frown. "This isn't normal, so tell me what's going on." His face blanches when I say the word *normal* but I can't take back my word choice now. I hate that I sound like such an asshole right now, but I can't seem to stop myself. It's a bad combination of being tired of lack of communication and being hopped up on my own hormones and adrenaline.

For a second, he hesitates like he's thinking about saying whatever it is but then shrugs his shoulders and holds his hands out helplessly. "It's not a big deal."

"Just tell me," I snap.

"Stop being like that." Now he's starting to get snappy, too. "I've put up with your shit, I don't think it's too much to ask that you return the favor."

I scoff. "At least you knew what my shit was. You're just leaving me to assume the worst—and I am by the way—assuming the worst right now." When he still doesn't say anything right away, I snap again, "What? Should I just leave? Some other girl that you actually want to sleep with is coming, and you can't risk me being here when she shows up?" I don't even know where that accusation comes from, but I put it out there anyway. *I need to chill the fuck out.*

Smith rolls his eyes at me but takes a step closer and runs his hand through my hair, resting his hand on the back of my head. "I love you. Stop being an asshole."

Conflicting feelings overwhelm me. My heart wants to go soaring, leaping, frolicking through meadows—but my head, my stubborn head, is mad that he's trying to do this right now. It doesn't feel good. Another boy telling me he loves me in the middle of a fight. As if it will somehow put a band-aid on everything. As if it magically fixes the problems.

I haven't forgotten the way I let the words slip out at the end of last school year, casually telling him

I loved him as we were parting ways. That's how I thought it would be when he said it. Natural. Sweet and unexpected, slipping out because he couldn't help himself. Not wielding the words like a shield in battle. There's nothing romantic about this, it just feels icky.

Smith lets out a long sigh and releases me. He puts his back to me again as he groans like he can't believe we're still talking about this. Finally, he says, "I have particular tastes, Jules. This—you and me here—*just us*, it uh, doesn't exactly check all my boxes."

I stare at his back for a long moment. I still don't get it. It doesn't exactly check all his boxes? What the hell else does he need? An audience? *Oh.* All those conversations last year had been relegated to the back of my mind but they jump back to the forefront now. He *does* need an audience. And not just an audience. He needs audience *participation*. He never tried to hide it from me. It was right there in plain sight. All those comments about Jax and Smith sharing girls.

"You and Jax—"

"Yeah," he cuts me off quickly.

"Oh my god. Do you *only* have sex with him involved?" My voice comes out nastier than I intended, especially because even though I sound disgusted by the idea, my lady bits are telling an entirely different story. I shift uncomfortably on the bed, trying to seek a little relief from the sudden pressure I feel between my legs.

Smith's whole face is bright red. He turns away from me, his shoulders tensed in a tight line that makes his dark navy t-shirt strain across his back. I didn't mean to be an asshole. And I didn't mean to embarrass him.

I knew he shared with Jax. That wasn't new information. I just didn't realize that's apparently *all* he does. He neglected to mention that one-on-one wasn't actually on the table. A horrible thought strikes me.

"So are we just never gonna be able to have sex?" My chest rises and falls in time with my short, irregular breaths. "Because it's never going to happen, Smith. You, me, and *Jax*." I'm trying to emphasize the point that Jax is the problem, but damn if I don't somehow miss the mark. He turns around, eyes blazing.

"Yeah, I get it. Two guys. Disgusting. Just get the fuck out then, Juliet."

"No, I—"

He interrupts me with an angry mutter. "Fine, I'll leave then." And I watch wide-eyed and open-mouthed as he storms out of his own bedroom, leaving me here in his bed alone. That didn't go how I thought it was going to go.

My first thought is to call him and explain that wasn't what I meant. My second thought is that I shouldn't fucking have to. He didn't give me a chance to explain. If he had only given me that, he would have realized that the heart of my concern was that I could never fully have him if I didn't accept Jax as part of the package deal. Even though I haven't been talking to the guys about it, I'm still hurting pretty bad over what happened with Jax. I've managed to play it cool—well, more like ice cold—with him when I've had to face him, but I've managed to keep my interactions with him to a minimum anyway.

Maybe if Smith was open to it just being someone other than Jax... I wasn't saying no. He should have stuck around to hear that, dammit. I'm tired of trying so hard all the time. This is the real reason so many people stick to monogamy. I'm barely struggling to stay afloat in one of these relationships, much less all of them.

This might all be a big mistake. Everything feels so fucked up right now.

I can't stay here in Smith's bed all day. I get up and go, sending a silent thank you prayer to the universe when I manage to make it out of the house without running into anyone else. It's like making a walk of shame without any of the perks but all of the shame.

19

The lunch table is silent as I take my seat. Ace shoots me a small smile, but apparently even he isn't willing to break the moody silence. I look over at Salma but she only shrugs. Sadie shakes her head and shrugs too. This is such bullshit.

Things with Jax were already weird, but it wasn't nearly so uncomfortable when it was only one person. Now, with issues still hanging in the air between Patrick and me, *and* Smith and me, the awkwardness is downright unbearable. I'm not going to start spending all my lunches like this. No fucking way. And at this rate, my relationships with these guys are gonna fall apart before they've even really had a chance to start.

"If I wanted to sit in silence I'd spend lunch in the library," I quip.

I'm surprised when it's Smith who snaps at me. "What the hell did you expect?"

"Why the fuck are you even mad, dude?" Patrick jumps in.

"None of your goddamn business." Smith glares at him.

Patrick scoffs. "You made it everybody's business by opening your fucking mouth."

"Whatever. Let me guess, you're whining again because for once you're not the golden boy at the center of everything."

"No, I'm mad because I'm not interested in playing third wheel while my girlfriend is fucking Woods."

"Wait, what?" Ace looks at me, confusion written all over his face. I'll admit, I assumed that Patrick had already spread that around our little group. Smith doesn't look surprised by the news, so I guess he already knew.

Ace glances down the table at Jax who snaps, "Don't even fucking look at me right now."

Ace chokes out a laugh. "I don't know why you're being an asshole to me. I spent all summer telling her to go easy on you."

"Oh, she went easy on him alright," Patrick mutters plenty loud enough for all of us to still hear him.

Jax is out of his seat before anyone can stop him. The whole cafeteria falls silent as Jax yanks Patrick up by the collar of his uniform shirt. "Throw the first punch, I dare you," Jax growls in his face.

"Oh, you'd like that, wouldn't you?" Patrick

glances over Jax's shoulder at me. "We all see how that turned out for you the last time."

I stand up, fully prepared to jump right into the middle as Jax shoves Patrick hard, sending him flying back several feet as he lands on his ass on the floor. Sadie grabs me by the elbow to stop me.

"Don't you dare step into the middle of that. Let the boys handle it," she tells me, nodding to where Ace and Smith are already coming around to break it up.

Patrick climbs back to his feet with pure, unfiltered anger in his eyes, directed at Jax. "What the fuck, Woods?" He takes a couple of steps forward but stops when he sees the rage on Jax's face. I try again to move towards them, but Sadie sticks her arm out. It wouldn't actually stop me if I wanted to go to them, but it's enough to stop me anyway. As much as I hate it, I know she's right. I can only make things worse by getting involved right now. Especially when I'm at the heart of this fight in the first place.

"Watch your goddamn mouth." Jax points an angry finger at him. He closes the distance so he can shove Patrick back again, but this time Patrick's ready for him and holds his ground. "You keep letting your ego do all the talking for you and she's going to get tired of dealing with your shit. I know I am."

"Like you're one to talk." Patrick looks at him with all the disgust he can seem to muster—which is a whole fucking lot. "Or have you forgotten how your first instinct after sex with the perfect girl was to gloat about how you had her first?"

An angry rumble breaks from Smith's chest. "You conveniently left that out when we spoke," he says, his voice low and furious. Ace is tense too, clearly just as angry to hear about what Jax said as anyone else.

So, basically, everyone is really fucking angry right now.

Everything is happening so fast, with way too much back and forth to follow. But if I thought the rest of the cafeteria was silent before, it's nothing compared to the actual silence that descends as the cafeteria door bursts open and Headmaster Dupont storms in. He stops a few feet away from the commotion—Jax and Patrick both heaving as they try to catch their breath. They're still eyeing each other like they might not be done fighting.

The headmaster stands with eyes blazing at the scene in front of him. I'm sure it doesn't escape anyone's notice that he glares at his son, in particular. "My office. Now," he snarls. To everyone else he shouts, "Lunch is over. Go to class."

Jax turns and walks right out. Privately, the headmaster says something to Patrick that no one else can hear. Patrick's shoulders droop as he responds, his eyes darting over to me. Already, I can see the apology forming in his eyes. I have to look away. I can't stomach seeing him looking that sorry after all the bullshit he just said. He said it all to hurt me, and this time it's way worse than anything he said when I first moved here. Because this time his words came from a place of angry honesty rather than insecurity. By the time I look back, Patrick is walking out with the headmaster hot on his heels.

I can only imagine how furious his dad must be with him. Aside from the fact that he already has insane expectations of his only child, this whole thing looks bad. The headmaster's son can't be fighting at school—especially not with the governor's son. The optics on that aren't good.

Now that the show is over, the spell over the rest of our classmates seems to be broken. Talking picks up again, a nervous chatter as people start to leave like Headmaster Dupont said.

I'm frozen in place as everyone else starts to stream out of the cafeteria. The gossip is swirling as people try to make sense of what just happened, and I can feel the stares as they pass by me. Ace, Sadie, and Salma all form a circle, trying to keep people from staring at me as I drop my head into my hands. I let out a shuddering breath, using up everything in me to keep from bursting into full-blown sobs right now. After just a second, I look up again, blinking rapidly up at the cafeteria lights as I try to swallow down all the emotion fighting to break free.

Salma looks at Ace and Sadie. "You two go ahead. I've got her." Ace looks like he's going to argue, but Sadie nudges him and makes him go. I mouth *thank you* to her. If I look at him, my sweet Ace, the one guy that I'm solid with right now, I know I'll fall apart for real. I wish it could be as easy to fix the rest of my problems as it was to strip down for Ace to fix the one I had with him.

Another minute passes with me trying not to cry in the now empty cafeteria as Salma rubs soothing circles over my back. She only stops when the actual bell for class chimes. "I'd offer to cut out of here with you and just skip the last two classes, but I think that would only make the talk worse."

"I know," I agree miserably. I'd like nothing more right now than to leave. Go home and curl up in my bed and try to forget this whole day ever happened. Or that any of it ever happened. Maybe I could create a little bubble for myself, an alternative universe where I returned to Patience but never bothered with school or friends or boys. Where I never asked questions and never had to face the ugly truths of where—and who—I came from.

No, I don't actually want that.

Salma walks side by side with me out into the hall. Luckily for me, Headmaster Dupont dismissing everyone from lunch early means most people have already gone back to class. The hallway is nearly empty, so there's no one to pretend for. I don't have to hide the misery I'm sure is written all over my face.

"I should check on them." I look towards the front office and even take a step in that direction, but Salma drags me right back.

"Woah. No way, girl. Stay far, far away from that mess right now. I'm sure Daddy Headmaster is livid with his little prince. You'll only make things worse."

"Can things really get any worse?" I ask.

Salma blows a breath out, her face sympathetic. "They can *always* get worse." She keeps her hand on me to walk me to class, as if she doesn't trust me to make it there on my own. We're nearing the door when she glances over with me with a sly grin. "I just have to say that I had no idea that was going to get so dramatic. Shouldn't multiple boyfriends—I don't know—entertain each other instead of fighting or something?"

"Of course not. That would be too damn easy," I grumble.

Ace is waiting for me when we reach the classroom. Salma lets go of me and I walk right into Ace's waiting arms. I feel hot tears burn behind my eyelids as I bury my face in his chest. We stand there like that for a long time. Longer than we're technically allowed. But when I walk into the classroom with bloodshot eyes and Ace with a tear-stained shirt, Mr. Bridges doesn't say a word about us being late. Thank fuck for small miracles.

20

I almost didn't agree to come tonight for two reasons, both of which I'm thinking about as Sadie and I walk up the driveway together. One, I'm still mad as hell at the guys—minus Ace, of course. Two, this is the same house where I started to feel things really shifting between Jax and me. Allie's house. The one with the fish tank room.

Sadie convinced me to come anyway. We spent the whole afternoon together, her trying to force me to relax as she ran me all over town for everything from new outfits to matching eyebrow waxes. It was nice, spending time with her despite the strain that still exists between us. It's hard not to feel like Salma took her place a little bit while Sadie was busy dealing with her addictions and lashing out at me when I know I didn't deserve it. Still, the longer she's sober, the more I start to remember why we became such close friends so fast in the first place.

We lose each other almost as soon as we get inside. The house is way more packed than last time. I hear some people mentioning they're from the prep school two towns over. Apparently, news of this party really spread.

I make a loop of the house, keeping my distance even when I catch glimpses of the guys. They don't seem to notice me, so I slip out of the room each time I stumble across one of them. I'm just not sure any of us are ready to talk. We've been avoiding each other since that scene in the cafeteria. Patrick and Jax both ended up suspended—turns out special privileges go out the window when it's the governor's son versus the headmaster's son.

Smith has been avoiding me. I can't even get him to take my calls so I can freaking apologize for our misunderstanding. The only one I've been okay with is Ace. He came and spent several evenings in a row sitting with me by Pearl's bedside.

It's gotten lonelier, spending time with Pearl at home. The nurses are quiet, trying to respect how much time Pearl spends sleeping now. It's good for Pearl, but hard on me.

It was nice to have some time with Ace there to keep me company. It made it hurt less when she didn't have any true lucid moments with me at all this week. Things have gotten so bad, and try as I might to distract myself, it's always lingering in the back of my mind. I don't know how much longer we have left. Weeks? Days? Hours? It makes me feel bad to be going out like this, even though I know it's what she really wants. I'm just terrified I won't be there for some stupid reason when the time comes.

I don't know why I'm getting so hung up on these thoughts right now. I can feel my face getting warm with the threat of tears. I get lucky and find Allie bee-lining straight for me at that moment.

"Hey!" I greet her. Her head jolts back in surprise as she offers an uncertain smile. I've never been the one to greet her first before. "It's crazy in here. I could use a minute alone. Do you think…?" I let my question trail off.

"God, yeah, of course." She reaches out and squeezes my hand like we're sharing *a moment*. I let her because even though I wouldn't consider us friends, asking for a favor isn't exactly the right moment to act like an asshole to someone. Allie points to the stairs. "Turn down the hallway at the end on your left and my bedroom is the last door on the right. It's off-limits to everyone else, so no one here will bother you."

"Thank you." I reach out and give her a quick hug that makes her face light up. She's being a real life-saver to me right now.

I follow her directions upstairs to the dark, empty room. It's even better than I expected, with a bathroom attached and everything. I splash cold water on my face, trying desperately to clear my mind even though I know there's no real chance of that.

I'm not in any real hurry to go back to the party. I walk back into the bedroom and let myself drop face first onto the bed, letting the bed muffle the strangled sound of frustration I let out. I catch myself wishing I could go back in time, but then remember that wouldn't solve anything. Different time, different problems. There's no point in time I could go back to where something wasn't problematic.

After I don't even know how long, I realize I probably need to go back out there. I haven't seen Salma yet and I'm sure she'll be looking for me. Ace, too.

I claw my way out of the comfort of the strange bed and say a silent goodbye to my brief haven. I'm admittedly a little distracted as I open the door to the hall. I pull the door closed and start to turn, smacking right into someone's chest.

"Sorry," I mumble as I take a step back. But then I look up and see who it is. "What are *you* doing here?"

Kareem smirks, leaning against the wall right outside the bedroom. "I'll admit I expected you to be a little more excited to see me."

"Then you're delusional," I retort, trying to brush past him.

He straightens to put his body in my way, blocking me in. I back up, reaching for the doorknob to the bedroom behind me. I don't have a good feeling about this. There's no one else in sight and the party's so loud that I don't know if I could even yell and be heard over the noise.

I don't understand why he's even here. This is a high school party. It's not at his house this time, so he's got no excuse for being here.

"Why so nervous?" he taunts me as he reaches out to brush the back of his hand against my cheek. I flinch, turning my head to the side. "Heard your little boyfriends got in quite the tussle. I'll bet you're feeling pretty lonely tonight."

"Why do you even know that?" *And why is he all up in my business?*

He shrugs. "Salma's loud when she's talking on the phone." I cringe inwardly as I think about all the raunchy conversations he's probably heard her side of over the past couple months. What a fucking creep.

There was a brief moment when I first saw him that I would have considered him attractive. Now when I look at him I have to try not to shudder. His vibe is completely off. The kind of guy I would have kept my distance from in Nikon Park. The kind of guy I want to keep my distance from here, except he keeps going out of his way to seek me out.

"I'm ready to go back to the party, Kareem." I gesture for him to let me pass. There's a calculated look in his eye as he gives me a wide grin.

"I don't think so," he purrs, taking a step closer so that I'm forced to put my back flat against the bedroom door to avoid making physical contact with him. It doesn't matter, he leans in anyway, erasing any sense of my personal space. I try to put a hand out to stop him but he bats it away.

"Kiss me," he demands, bringing his mouth within inches of mine. I tilt my head down and to the side so there's no easy way for him to close the distance.

"No." My voice is hoarse.

He slams his hand against the door dangerously close to my head. I flinch and turn my face the other way. *Why didn't I just stay downstairs with everyone else?* This isn't like the game of cat and mouse I played with Jax. There's something dark about Kareem. It's the way he stares at me like an object instead of a person. There's no playing chicken with Kareem, because I have no way of knowing what lines he's willing to cross.

There's no way in hell I'm going to kiss him. I glance down, trying to gauge whether I could just knee him in the balls and run.

He glances down and understanding dawns on his face. "Try it," he warns, "And I'll fuck you so hard you'll be lucky if you can walk out of here on your own."

I swallow hard, trying to tamp down the fear that rises up my throat. It's clear I don't want to have sex with him—it's also obvious he doesn't care. He's making sure I know that's a line he's willing to cross. He wants me to be afraid of him. I'm sure he thinks fear will make me more pliant. The joke's on him.

I've already had a lifetime of fear thrown at me. The only thing fear can do is make me focus.

Maybe there's no playing chicken with Kareem but there's still an advantage to catching him off guard. I make sure my fingers are clasped around the cool metal of the doorknob and I force my body to visibly relax.

"That's better," he murmurs. He reaches out and strokes my cheek again, letting his hand drop to work a path down my chest so he can cop a good feel. I hope he fucking enjoys it because it's the last chance he's going to get to touch me.

As he starts to lean in to try to kiss me, I turn the doorknob and shove it open, turning and darting into the room as Kareem stumbles. He's quick to regain his balance, a snarl on his face as he steps into the room and slams the door closed behind him. My heart is slamming against my ribcage, and I know I'm taking a real risk now that we're behind a closed door, but this is my one chance.

He creeps towards me, his body tensed like a wild animal as he stalks me across the room. I take two steps for one of his, but it doesn't matter. His steps are bigger than mine. It doesn't take long for him to be within reach.

"Don't act like you don't like it like this. You've fucked Jax Woods and I know all about his reputation. Don't worry, though." He grins. "I like it rough, too. The rougher the better. Which means the more you fight me, the sweeter it's going to be when I'm inside of you." The very idea of that disgusts me and I don't bother hiding it.

Kareem's grin widens. "None of your bitch ass boyfriends are here to save you now." He takes another step forward and I take one backward, my back finally hitting the wall. I slide my left hand out, fingers brushing the thing I noticed when I first came in here.

I jerk my chin up. "I don't need anyone else to save me."

My words make him laugh, but I only smile sweetly back at him. Because I know something he doesn't. Allie Townsend plays softball.

He screams like a fucking baby when the bat hits his knee. I wish it had been his dick I was swinging out, but I needed a much bigger target than the tiny prick I'm sure this guy has. "Fucking bitch," he snarls, but that wasn't his best move. I swing the bat again, wincing when this time there's the unmistakable crack of the hit doing real damage. I'm not sure if it's to the bat or Kareem's bones—and I'm not interested in sticking around to find out.

I drop the bat and move faster than I ever have in my life, wrenching the door open and sprinting towards the sound of people. I'm not even to the steps yet when I slam into Patrick.

"Woah." He grabs my shoulders to steady me and must see the panic on my face. "What's going on?

Are you okay?" He's frenzied as he looks me over but I know there's nothing for him to see except my shaking body.

There's no way for me to avoid it—I break into full-on, total meltdown sobs. I try to open my mouth to speak but I can't get a word out. He pulls me to him and squeezes me so tight I can barely breath. "You're freaking me out, Juliet. What's going on?" I take a deep, shuddering breath and try to squeeze words out of my painfully dry throat.

"Kareem. He—" I can't even fucking say it. "I hit him. With. A bat," I whimper out in between sobs.

Patrick goes almost scarily calm as he puts his hands on my shoulders and pulls away to look at me again. "Did he hurt you?" he asks solemnly. I pause, but then shake my head no. "Did he try to?" he growls. I nod. He lets go of me, his eyes looking over my shoulder toward the hallway I came out from. "Go get Jax."

I try to protest but the only thing that comes out of me is a blubbering sound and more tears. I can't get the image of Jax shoving Patrick out of my head. I want him to ask for someone else, but Patrick peers into my eyes with a heavy, pointed look.

"I saw him out back a few minutes ago. Go get him, Juliet. Send him up here. And then go find someone to take you home."

"No!" I manage to choke out. I'm not leaving. Especially not if something bad is about to happen. I need to know that everyone is okay. Patrick reads the desperation in my face and nods. "Find Ace or Smith. Have them take you out to wait in the car. Don't come back inside until one of us comes to get you. Do you understand?"

I nod. It's a compromise I can live with.

Patrick watches me reach the stairs before he turns and heads for the other hall. It takes everything in me not to turn back, to tell him it's not worth it. That I don't want him getting in trouble again because of me. But Patrick is a lot calmer than I am right now, at least on the surface, and he told me to get Jax.

People stare as I shove my way through the crowd, fighting my way to the back door. Several people try to stop me to ask if I'm okay but I ignore them, refusing to be deterred from my search. A wave of panic washes over me when I step outside and see how many people there are everywhere. I turn my head desperately from side to side, hoping against all reason to catch a glimpse of him. I'm almost ready to give up and just collapse in on myself when something catches my eye. Someone is standing by themselves at the edge of the yard.

My feet are moving before I'm really even sure it's him. "Jax," I croak out his name as I get close. He starts to turn and I fling myself at him. He manages to catch me just in time to keep us both from ending sprawled out on the ground.

For a split second, his arms are tight around me,

stroking my back as he holds me close. Then a sob breaks free and he freezes up.

He slowly lets go of me, stepping back to get a good look at my face for the first time. He couldn't when I was throwing myself at him, but now he sees what an emotional wreck I am—and he sees the tears. "What the fuck happened?" he demands.

"Salma's brother." God, I wish I could stop shaking. "Patrick told me to find you. He wants you to come upstairs. To Allie's bedroom." All the words come out disjointed a little bit scrambled, but Jax doesn't question any of it. His eyes glance towards the house as if he could look through walls to see what's happening upstairs.

Jax cups his hands around and his mouth and yells, "Smith!" And within seconds, Smith is headed our way. His eyes guarded as he crosses the yard towards us. Jax is too impatient for him to wait to reach us, he sets off toward the house, then pauses and turns back. I don't know what he's doing as he stomps back to me until his mouth meets mine, claiming me with a hard kiss that's packed with emotion. I let him, too, even though I'm not sure I'm done being mad at him.

"What's going on?" Smith asks as he reaches us and Jax starts to push past him. He doesn't get an answer.

"Stay with her," Jax barks out, leaving us together in the yard.

I try to blink back the tears that won't seem to

stop as Smith crushes me against his chest. "I probably don't want to know," he says quietly, not bothering to ask again about what's happening. He whispers into my ear, telling me everything is okay, his voice soothing me until the tears stop coming. I hiccup as I pull in a deep breath.

"Patrick told me to have you or Ace take me to the car," I manage to tell him. "And to stay there until him or Jax say so."

Smith nods without question. "That's what we're doing then, come on." He tucks me under his arm, squeezing me tightly to him so that there's not an inch of space left between our bodies. He pulls me over to the group of people standing closest to us. He turns to one of the guys. "Hey, can you find Asher and tell him to meet me at my car?"

The guy nods. "Yeah, man. Of course."

Smith thanks him, then starts pulling me back the other way again. "Where are we going?" I ask quietly as he pulls me around to the side of the house.

"There's no way in hell we're going back in the house right now. We can go around the side here and get to my car on the street. This way we probably won't run into anyone, okay?" I sag with relief. Avoiding other people right now is exactly what I want to do.

Smith deposits me safely in the passenger seat of his car before walking around to the driver's side. He doesn't get in right away and when I peek out I see why. Ace is jogging our way. That guy must have found him awfully fast. My head feels like it's swimming as I watch him and Smith talk for a minute outside the car before joining me inside. It's a good thing Smith's in this car and not his sports car, I muse aimlessly to myself as Ace tucks himself into the backseat.

Smith turns the music in his car to a radio station he knows I like and turns it up so that the sound tunes out the lingering sounds of the party. He offers me his hand, which I take, and then Ace leans forward and offers me his hand, which I also take. The three of us sit like that, hands clasped until Patrick shows up sometime later. I don't even have any concept of how much time has passed. My brain is so scrambled.

Smith uses his free hand to unlock the car doors for Patrick, and Patrick slide into the backseat next to Ace. I lean over to examine him, surprised that there's not so much as a wrinkle in his shirt, much less any sign of a fight. Smith turns the music down so we don't have to try to talk over it.

"What happened?" I ask quietly, wanting to prepare myself.

"Word's already spread. Let's just say Jax and I weren't the only ones interested in *taking care of it*."

I glance out the window but no one else is coming. "Where's Jax?" I ask.

Patrick seems reluctant to tell me but he caves

when I start to breathe like I might start hyperventilating. I can only imagine the worst. That's why Jax isn't here, isn't it—because something's really wrong? Patrick reaches over the seat to rub my shoulder in a reassuring gesture. "He was having a little harder time walking away. Some guys walked him out back to cool down. I'm sure he's coming. He'll lose his mind if he doesn't get to check on you himself."

"Did someone call the cops?" Ace asks.

Patrick shakes his head. "Someone heard the commotion and got Salma. She called her parents before we could call the police. Based on the part of the call we heard—that was probably worse." He leans forward. "She was worried about you. I told her we'd take care of you tonight and then you could call her tomorrow. Okay?"

I nod gratefully.

Someone knocks on the window and I nearly jump out of my skin. "Sorry," Jax says, his words muffled from outside the car. I let go of Ace and Smith so I can fling the door open, nearly hitting him. He steps out of the way just in time. My eyes scan every inch of him but there aren't any marks on him either. I let out a breath I didn't realize I was holding.

"Here." Jax holds his hand out to me as if to help me out of the car. All three the guys start to protest at once but Jax waves his other hand at them, wordlessly telling them to cut it out. I don't know why he's having me get out but I take his hand anyway.

I'm confused as he switches me positions and takes my seat in the car. He takes my hand again, tugging me back toward the car. *He wants me to sit in his lap.* I'm not sure how good of an idea that really is but I don't have the energy to fight. I climb in, surprised when Jax puts his hand behind my head to keep me from hitting it on the roof of the car. He pulls the car door closed behind me and spreads his legs a little wider so I can sit across them comfortably. It's only awkward for a few seconds before I'm sinking against him, the weight of what happened making my body too weary to hold myself up any longer.

He wraps one arm around my legs and strokes my side with the other. We're back to not talking and Smith turns the music up again.

A fresh wave of tears hits me like a brick wall. I turn my face into Jax's shoulder as I blindly reach out with one hand, not even sure whose hand it is that takes mine and holds it as I cry. For a long time we all just sit there while they let me cry. I'm not even sure if they know yet what exactly happened, and I know that I'm not even remotely ready to try to explain. The only thing that matters right now is that they were there. All of them. Even though three of the four were mad at me for some reason or another, tonight we all came back together. And I don't want to let any of them go ever again.

That night, they all come home with me. For once I'm glad when Pearl doesn't wake up when I get home, so that I don't have to explain why four guys end up sleeping on makeshifts pallets on the floor surrounding my bed.

21

Three of the four guys are still asleep on the floor when I wake up early the next morning. The curtains are drawn, so it's too dark to see who's missing. My brain goes fuzzy when I try to remember who laid down where last night. I carefully pull the covers back and tiptoe around the bodies, slipping out of the bedroom and closing the door back quietly behind me.

My footsteps are silent as I tread downstairs to check on Pearl. When I turn the corner into the sitting room, the first thing I notice is that the nurse is sitting off to the side with a book. My first thought is that Pearl must be asleep, but that's not the case. I'm surprised to see she's up and alert, Patrick leaning back in a chair by her bedside, smiling easily as she says something to him. They don't notice me, so I don't announce myself.

I lean against the doorframe, watching how

easily Patrick talks to her, rambling on about something that happened in Patience years before he was ever even born. He looks completely at ease at her bedside.

He's the first to notice me, glancing up sharply as if he suddenly just felt me in the room with him. There's a spark in his eyes as he smiles across the room at me, never breaking the conversation with Pearl. They go on for a few more minutes before she notices me.

"Ah, Juliet." Pearl's eyes light up as they settle on me. "Come in and join us. If you don't, I might just decide to steal this one from you." She reaches out to pat Patrick's hand affectionately.

I let out a soft groan, horribly embarrassed to hear her saying something like that. She tilts her chin up, looking affronted by my horror.

"What? It's not like you don't have more. You could spare at least one." She sounds so matter-of-fact when she says it that I barely manage to hold back a laugh.

Patrick raises his eyebrows at me as I'm sure my cheeks turn bright red. He seems surprised to hear Pearl so casually referring to my having multiple boyfriends. I'll have to catch him up to speed later when we're out of earshot of my elderly and partially senile aunt. I can only imagine what else she might come up with to say otherwise.

I pull a chair up next to Patrick and sit down,

reaching for his hand. He turns it over to lace his fingers with mine and squeezes.

There's a silent question in his eyes as he looks at me. A question he can't ask in front of Pearl. *Are you okay?* "I got a good night's sleep," I tell him out loud, hoping that's enough to answer his question. I still don't feel great, but I slept well knowing my guys were there with me.

"That's nice, dear," Pearl says patronizingly. Patrick barely conceals a soft laugh under his breath.

We sit for a while, Pearl and Patrick returning to their talk about the history of our town as I sit just enjoying the sounds of their voices. He talks to her until she starts to drift in and out, and then the nurse asks us to step out so she can do some of the ickier parts of her job before Pearl is completely out of it again. She doesn't have to ask me twice. It only took one time for me to learn I didn't want to be in the room for any of that stuff if I can help it.

Patrick keeps hold of my hand as we leave the room and cross down the hall to the kitchen. We sit down at the little table in the breakfast nook off to the side of the kitchen, sitting in side-by-side chairs so that we never have to let go of each other. It might actually be the first time I've actually sat down here since moving in. I would have sat here a lot more if I'd realized what a great view of the back-yard it has.

"Do you want to talk about last night?" Patrick asks me.

"Honestly?" I shake my head. "I'd like to talk about literally anything but that."

"What about us? Can we talk about that?" he asks, an uncertainty in his voice that makes my chest ache. I don't want him to think he can't talk to me. Not talking is what got us into trouble in the first place. We've got to move past that. Last night really showed me what I'm not willing to walk away from —what I'm not willing to lose.

I shift so I can face Patrick a little more head on. "Yes. A million times yes."

"I'm sorry about taking you up to Churchill Point and acting like a jackass. Jax wasn't so far off base. I've always been the kid hearing people tell me I could have anything I wanted, so it's not all that easy when suddenly the one thing I want feels just out of reach. It's not the sharing that gets to me. It's that I feel like I keep getting knocked down into last place every time someone new steps in."

I let go of his hand and his face falls, but not for long as I lay my palms flat on his cheeks, squeezing his face a little. *Don't get distracted by how hot he is right now, Juliet.* "I don't feel that way at all. You're not last place to me. Not ever."

His eyes are soft and warm on mine. "I love you, Juliet. And not because we're arguing and I want it to stop, or because I'm worried someone else will get to say it first. I love you, and I want you to love me back."

"Of course I love you back, you idiot." I tug his

face closer so I can kiss him properly. Overjoyed when this kiss is like the ones from before, not anything like the cheap knockoff I got when we were fighting at Churchill Point. This is perfect. This is everything. All the heartache of these past weeks dissipates as we kiss while the sun rises over the horizon.

Smith's voice interrupts us. "Jules?"

We both turn to see the guys standing in the doorway, Jax hanging back slightly from Ace and Smith. I stay where I'm at. The urge to move I might have felt before is gone. We're one team. One unit. And now I know it's okay if the others see me with one of them. It's like Smith told me in the first place, it's all about being honest.

No one seems bothered. Ace and Smith squeeze into seats at the table with us, but Jax hangs back by the doorway. "Come sit," I invite him softly.

He doesn't move. Doesn't speak either. I can see it in his eyes that he feels like the odd man out now that the dust has settled from last night. He was an asshole—*is* an asshole—but as far as I'm concerned right now, he's *my* asshole. Patience might be all about every man for himself, but I'm not. We're a group, and we care about each other, and I know Jax belongs as part of that whether he's willing to agree or not. Even assholes can't survive life alone. Especially not life in Patience, where I'm learning it's not enough to think you're being careful of who you trust. You basically need a signed letter of recommendation to know for sure.

"I can go," he says finally. It's not the same as saying he wants to go, it's that he thinks that's really going to be what I want.

"Don't go, Jax." It's so silent in here as the guys wait to see how this one ends. "Please."

He moves at glacier speed towards the table, as if he thinks I'm going to change my mind and he shouldn't bother hurrying along. He takes the seat between Smith and Ace, sitting across from me and holding my eyes the whole time. That's enough for me right now. He's at the table. We don't have to decide what it means just yet, I'm just glad he's here.

Later, I'll have to talk about a lot of things—like what happened last night. But that's later, and this is now. And for now, the only thing I want to think about is how much I love these boys. *My boys.*

22

They think I don't know what they're doing, but it's been obvious all week. The guys have hovered around me, basically taking shifts of who's with me at any given time so that I barely ever get a second alone. Sometimes, I'm lucky enough to get them all at once. We've watched more movies in a week than I think I watched in the whole rest of the year combined.

Tonight though, it's just me and Jax. His parents are away at some political charity thing, so the whole house is ours. Not that we need it, since we go straight to his room anyway.

I take up a spot on his bed, leaning back into his pillows as he watches me, his Adam's apple bobbing as he swallows hard. I pat the other side of the bed. "Come lay with me." He indulges me, coming to join me on the bed, and I roll over so that I can rest my head on his chest. His arm naturally comes up around me, his hand resting on my lower back. We lay like that for a few minutes as I just enjoy a moment of calm. It's been a long freaking week. So many people wanted to bombard me with questions, and Salma was apologizing every time I turned around as if she was personally responsible for her monster of a brother. It's all just been exhausting.

"What the fuck are we doing?" Jax breaks the silence.

I think he's talking about our relationship at first, but then I realize how stiff he feels under me. "Cuddling?" I say like it's a question, glancing up at him with serious confusion. *I'll bet Jax Woods has never cuddled before.* I have to look away before he notices the smug look I get when I realize that.

"I fucking hate it," he says, but I notice he holds me a little tighter. He can say whatever he wants— he's a surprisingly good cuddle buddy.

"Tell me about your dad," I say as I shift even closer to him. He tenses up again, but I throw my arm over his midsection and feel him relax once more. "The two of you don't seem close," I add, wanting him to know why I'm bringing it up. I don't want to seem like I actually give a crap who his dad is, past the natural curiosity about their weirdly strained relationship.

"He's not my dad."

I shoot up, Jax wincing as I elbow him on accident in my hurry to get where I can look down into his face. I'm leaning half over him as I look expectantly at him, waiting for an explanation. He can't just drop a bomb like that and not explain it.

Jax twirls some of my hair around his finger. "We have the house to ourselves. Are you sure talking about my dad is really what you want to do right now?"

"Yeah," I answer, a challenge in my eyes. A relationship means talking. So, if that's what we're doing here, I need to know he's all in. I open my mouth to tell him as much, but he starts talking before me.

"My mother cheats a lot. It's probably the worst kept secret in all Patience really. It's always been like that. Mom sleeps with someone from town. Dad sleeps with an employee. It's fifty different kinds of fucked up, but it's the relationship they chose." He lets go of my hair to grab my hand and bring it up to his lips. I'm surprised when he kisses the back of my hand. This is a much softer side of him I'm seeing, and it actually makes me more nervous than I would have expected. *Shit is getting real.*

"So, Governor Woods—"

"Isn't my biological dad." He nods, confirming it. "I'm the bastard child he's stuck with. It would have been political suicide for him to do anything but claim me. Not even necessarily because of the cheating, but because my real father is a man that got framed for tax crimes." He grits his teeth through the next part. "And Governor Woods is the man that refused to pardon him, right after he found out the man had slept with his wife."

Hearing those sharp words he uses to describe himself and the circumstances of his paternity makes my heart hurt for him. I knew there was something not right in his family, but I never would have guessed this. I stay quiet, letting him tell me more at his own pace. I've started to understand how he is, so I know he doesn't want to show it, but this has to be hurting him more than he's letting on.

"When I'm getting away with shit all the time? It's because he bails me out to buy my silence. He's got bigwig political opponents on every side of the aisle, but it's his teenage bastard child that really scares the hell out of him—because he knows I could bring his whole political empire crashing down with barely a snap of my fingers."

"Jax," I say his name softly. This is so damn hard to listen to. "I'm sorry." I get the feeling this isn't something he's talked about often, or maybe not even at all. I ask him, "Would you really ever do that to him?"

His eyes go dark. "Let's hope I never have to actually give you an answer to that."

I lay my head back on his chest, digesting everything he's just told me. I didn't actually expect him to be so open and honest with me. All week, I've been noticing he's a little less rough around the edges when it comes to me, but this is still unexpected.

We go back to a peaceful silence, his exposed secret now hanging in the air between us. I let my eyes wander, studying his room more closely than I did when I've been in here before. I peek over at his bookshelf, squinting to see if he's read anything interesting. There's a book on the second shelf that certainly draws my attention.

"What's up?" he asks as I get up and leave him in bed alone.

"This book," I answer, not explaining any further than that. I take it off the shelf and open it, already pretty certain about what I'm going to find. *It is not down on any map; true places never are.* Right there at the front of the inside cover, just like the other two books. Is it possible Hollis was blackmailing the governor? That he sent Ed Woods this book for the same reason he sent one to Francis Van Doren?

"Have you seen this before?" I turn to ask Jax. He gives me a strange look as he stands up and comes over to join me. He's probably wondering why I'm grabbing something off his shelf and then asking if he's *seen* it. Of course he's *seen* it, but the real answer I'm looking for is bigger than that. I want to know if he knows why Hollis would have sent his dad this book?

"Yeah, of course. Hollis gave me that as a kid. The last birthday I had before he died, I think. I was mad as hell too, but my mom made me keep it because she said it would be rude not to." *So, the book wasn't for Ed at all, but for Jax.* He runs his hand over the cover. "Why?"

"No reason," I lie, telling myself that it's just a little white lie and that it's okay because I fully

240

intend to tell him the truth later. Just not until I've talked to Smith. And then we can decide the best way to tell the others. This book—and this quote— they have to mean something. Something important. This can't be a coincidence. "I love old books." That part's not a lie, I reason.

I put the book back on the shelf, trying to ignore the suspicious way Jax watches me walk back over to plop down on his bed. He knows I'm not giving him the whole truth, but I'm hoping he'll let it go for just a little longer.

"Come here." I beckon him back to the bed.

"More cuddling?" he asks, a little bit of dread seeping into his voice.

"No." I shake my head. "No more cuddling." I raise an eyebrow, waiting for him to get on the same page with me. He comes to the bed and grabs me by my ankle, pulling me slightly down the bed and forcing me to fall onto my back. A nervous giggle slips out.

He comes up and settles over me, rolling his hips against mine in a teasing way that makes me whole body shudder with pleasure. He slips his hand up my shirt to touch me as he starts to kiss me. Things start to escalate quickly, which is no surprise with Jax. He tugs at my hair the way I like so fucking much, and then nibbles at the base of my neck before kissing me on the mouth again. We stay like that for several minutes, but as my body starts to plead for more, there's an idea forming in the back of my mind.

"Jax?" I mumble his name against his lips.

"Hmm?"

I pull back slightly. "What if... What if I said there was something I wanted to do for Smith?"

I bite down on my bottom lip, wondering what the hell I'm getting myself into as I notice the glint in Jax's eyes.

23

The moment Smith lets himself into the room couldn't have been better timing if I'd planned it. He walks in to me sitting on the edge of Jax's bed, Jax stalking towards me from across the room as he's getting tired of waiting. We both turn toward the door as it opens, all three of us suddenly looking like deer caught in headlights.

"Oh." That's all Smith says.

Jax walks over to close the bedroom door behind him as Smith takes a few uncertain steps further into the room. I can't read his expression. Can't tell if he has some idea why Jax called him here.

Jax raises his eyebrows at me from behind Smith, the message clear. I asked for this. He's expecting me to take the lead now. *Great.* I'm the only one of us that doesn't have experience with this. God, I can feel my whole body break out into a light sweat. Can I actually do this?

If I don't, I'm going to lose Smith. That's reason enough to try.

I stand up on unsteady feet. I wish in this moment I could be a lot of things. Calm, collected, sexy—but the reality is that I'm as intimidated as hell. I take a few steps toward Smith before I freeze up. I don't know how to do this. What if someone starts to feel left out? Or if it's better with one person than the other? What if I can't handle two guys at once? The questions I can't answer for myself leave me paralyzed.

Jax softens for me when he sees the panic in my eyes. He closes the distance, stepping in behind Smith close enough that they're almost touching. Smith stiffens and glances back over his shoulder at him before looking back at me. His brows furrow with confusion, understanding not quite dawning on him. I can't blame him. After the way I freaked out on him, he probably doesn't even realize this is an option.

"Come here," Jax says, beckoning me closer.

I move towards them as if a rope is pulling me in, absolutely no conscious thought required. Smith glances over his shoulder at Jax again, but Jax doesn't acknowledge it. When I'm close enough, Jax reaches around Smith to deftly work the buttons on my shirt open with one hand. He's slow about it. So slow I'm tempted to tell him to hurry the fuck up. All my clothes suddenly feel too hot. Too tight. Too in the way.

I'm not sure Smith is even still breathing at this point, his eyes following Jax's hand as it works a trail down the front of my shirt. When the last button comes undone, Jax drops his hand.

Smith finally seems to find his voice, dragging his eyes away from where my shirt is now hanging open. "You don't have to do this, Jules." He glances at Jax again. "I don't want her doing this because you made her feel like she had to." Smith frowns and there's a serious sadness to his eyes, like he really thinks my willingness in this is an impossibility.

"Give us both a little fucking credit." Jax rolls his eyes, stepping out from behind Smith so they can actually face each other. "This wasn't *my* idea."

"I—What?" Smith chokes out as they both turn to look at me.

I never took a second to consider what having them both in the same room together like this would look like, but *damn.* Jax, with his dark features, and Smith, with his lighter ones, the contrast between them stirs something in me. It's like someone invited my own personal angel and devil into this room and told me I didn't have to choose.

I can't find words of my own. So, I go with actions instead. With calculated slowness, I ease my shirt off my shoulders, letting the material flutter to the floor. It's so quiet in here a pin could drop and we'd probably all jump out of our skin.

Fuck, I should have asked Jax to turn the air conditioning up or something. I feel like my whole body is catching fire from the inside out. If I'm this overheated already, I'm not sure I can make it through whatever's about to happen without actually combusting. Which is made all the worse when Jax grabs the back of his own shirt and tugs it over his head. Smith and I both stare at him for a minute, and honestly at this point I might actually be more into this than Smith is.

"Are you sure about this?" he asks, turning back to me with concern clear in his eyes.

I step closer to him, grabbing the hem of his shirt in my hands. "Please," I say as I start to lift, "Stop fucking talking." And then I pull his shirt over his head so that now both guys are only half-dressed. I can feel my eyelids droop as I look back and forth between the two of them. They're both so distractingly hot that it's hard to decide where to focus my eyes.

Somehow, that turns into my gaze dipping down, checking out the below the belt situation. I can tell immediately how turned on they both are, and that helps most of my uncertainty dissipate. There are no wrong answers here, I realize. All the same things are hot—just doubled.

I take advantage of my proximity to Smith, leaning into him as I tug his head down to mine so I can kiss him. There's no easing into it, as far as I'm considered it's full steam ahead the second our lips brush. I open my mouth to him, letting our tongues tangle as I feel the heat of Jax's body come up behind me. He runs his hands up over my ass as I kiss his friend. He doesn't stop there. He presses his thumbs into my back, eliciting a soft moan from me as he massages his way all the way up my spine.

Smith reacts to the sound by kissing me harder and then Jax is brushing my hair away from the back of my neck and pressing his lips between my shoulders. The feel of it makes my back arch, the front of me pushing harder against Smith as my ass presses back against Jax.

"There's too many clothes," I mumble in between kissing Smith.

Jax chuckles as he slides his hands around my midsection and then drags them down to the waistband of my jeans. "I agree," he murmurs as he snaps open the button of my jeans. Smith's mouth leaves mine as he tilts his head down to watch as Jax tells me, "Take them off."

No one has to tell me twice. This time, there's nothing slow about the way I strip down. I yank the jeans down my legs as fast as I can, feeling the guys' eyes on me as I bend over, my ass on display for Jax as my cleavage is on display for Smith. When I stand back up, I look from one to the other.

"Your turn." My voice comes out huskier than it ever has, raspy from the effort it takes to talk through the mouth watering that's happening as I admire how goddamn hot these guys both are. And right now, all of that's for me. Every inch of them. *If this is the trade-off I get for all the bullshit life has thrown at me, I'll fucking take it.*

I step back as the guys both shuck their pants, that way I can watch them both at once. Jax glances from Smith to me, and then pulls his briefs over his hips, too, leaving himself completely exposed to the both of us. And even though I've already had sex with Jax, it's like I'm seeing him for the first time. I only manage to tear my eyes away when Smith follows suit, pulling his boxers down and stepping out of them.

They're both naked. I'm in a bedroom with two naked guys. Holy shit. A darker look comes over Jax's face as he stalks towards me.

He grabs a fistful of my hair as his other hand splays across my lower back, jerking me closer to him. His mouth descends on mine, kissing me so hard it's almost painful as he uses my hair to tug me this way and that—however he wants me. I try to keep up but it's impossible. He kisses me like he's really only using my mouth for his own pleasure and I can start to feel an uncomfortable feeling building between my legs. I shift in place, trying to rub my thighs together, and Jax pulls back to frown at me.

He makes me turn, putting my back to his front again, and makes me jump slightly when he cups me with his hand through the front of my underwear. "Do you feel that?"

I nod even though I'm feeling a lot of things and I

have no idea which thing he's talking about. I shudder as his breath blows across my ear.

"You're not in charge anymore, do you understand?" I nod, goosebumps prickling up all over my body. "The only relief you get is if one of us decides to give it to you." My breath catches as I keep nodding like an idiot.

Jax lets go of me, giving me a gentle shove that lands me in Smith's arms. He stares down at me with all the reverence of someone that really cares for me. I don't even need to hear the words because I see them clear as day. He loves me. Which makes this whole thing that much sweeter. I love him, too, even though I know this isn't the right moment to say it. Not that I need to anyway, no, right now is all about *showing not telling.*

Smith puts a hand on my hip to lead me backwards, walking me towards the bed until the backs of my knees hit the mattress. I let myself fall back onto the plush bed, looking up at Smith as he climbs over me, his hips sliding excruciatingly against me as his hard-on teases my body. It's a promise of what's to come. Remembering Jax's words, I fight not to rub against Smith like a goddamn cat in heat.

Down, girl. The boys are in charge.

"I'm still wearing too many clothes," I whisper up to him.

He starts to answer but a rattling noise startles me. I look over to find Jax dragging a chair closer to the bed. His eyes find mine, unwavering as he sits down and leans back casually, making himself comfortable with quite the view.

"Undress her," Jax instructs Smith while never taking his eyes off of me.

Smith is all too happy to oblige. He dips his fingers into the sides of my panties, drawing the black material down my legs with excruciating slowness. I raise my hips for him, and when the fabric passes my knees, he moves so his mouth can reach my thighs—kissing the top of one and then the other. He slides my panties the rest of the way off and then undoes my bra and flings it away. I'm certain things are going to kick into high gear, but Smith moves back between my legs to kiss my thighs again, his mouth working from the outside of my thighs to the inside. My body quivers in anticipation.

When his lips touch dangerously close to my center I nearly come up off the bed. He chuckles, the sound rattling me as his mouth vibrates against the inside of my thigh.

I'm not even remotely ready for the moment he tastes me. I don't know where to put my hands, trying—and failing—to keep them from grasping the back of his head. I don't know where to put my eyes either at first, but then they land on Jax, watching him as he watches Smith. I can see him getting hard as he watches, and when he realizes I'm watching him he starts to stroke himself.

I like that he's watching. I even like that he's touching himself.

It isn't long before I'm desperately tugging at Smith's hair, wanting him to continue but also stop at the same time. I need more. But he doesn't stop until he's good and ready. And by that point, I'm coming completely undone. I throw my head back as a whole range of sounds come out of me. Within seconds, I feel spent.

That doesn't stop my toes from curling as Smith starts to kiss his way up my body, paying special attention to my chest before working his way up the side of my neck.

I can't take much more of this. Everything is too heightened. Like every single one of my senses is on high alert. My body tenses as Jax stands up and strolls closer to the bed. Smith glances over at him and then rolls to the side, grabbing my hip to roll me over with him so that we're facing each other. It's a good thing we're laying down because I don't think my legs could hold me up as Jax gets on the bed and presses himself up against my back. I can feel every inch of him, including his dick as it nestles up against my ass. *Thank fuck for king-sized beds.*

Smith's mouth finds mine as Jax skims his hand up the side of my body I get so caught up in Smith kissing me that I don't get the chance to notice Jax's mouth moving over my shoulder until he sinks his teeth into my skin, making me lurch one way and then the other as my body seeks out the contact it needs.

They both press closer, sandwiching me between

them. And holy hell, are four hands better than two as they both take their time with my body. It's hell trying to be even somewhat still as their two totally different styles of touching meld together. For every time I wince from Jax's rough handling of me, Smith is there soothing the pain.

Something weird happens as the minutes pass like this, I start to *see it*. The way the two of them are so close, and the way Smith naturally defaults to him. It's because they're so in tune with what the other needs. I've never met two people more able to balance each other.

Jax is the first to pull away, his body heat abandoning me for a moment as a drawer opens and closes. I can't help but tense up, uncertain of exactly how this next part goes. There's a part of me that's worried I won't like it when it actually comes down to going all the way. I don't know who's going where or how, and that anxiety makes me stiff.

"Relax," Jax growls at me as he nips the skin at the base of my neck. He sounds so much like how he did the first time we did this, and it's that memory that convinces me to let go. Jax didn't fail me the first time around. I have to trust that him and Smith are going to take care of me this time too.

Jax reaches over me, and I watch as he hands Smith a condom. I think that answers my question about what happens next—until I hear the unmistakable crinkle of Jax opening a wrapper behind me.

Jax pushes me onto my back again, but holds

himself back, propping his elbow up on the bed as he rests his head against his hand. Smith's the one that climbs back over me, his mouth finding mine as he nudges my legs farther apart. Jax must not think it's far enough, because I distinctly feel his hand grab my thigh and pull me open even more.

When Smith presses into me for the first time, it's instant bliss. He takes his time, completely unhurried as he explores all the different sounds and reactions I make as he tests the waters. *He's adapting.* I've never experienced anything quite like it. He doesn't just go all in, he takes the time to note exactly what I need, more in tune with my body than anyone has ever been. He discovers things I didn't even know I liked, like the certain swivel of his hips that strokes inside of me in a way that makes me jolt.

He's too good. I don't last any time at all before I'm moaning out my release, one arm clasped around his back as my other hand somehow ending up against Jax's chest. He isn't far behind me, clearly a pro at good timing.

By the time he relieves me of his body weight, both of us completely spent for the moment, I realize I've got a few stray tears in my eyes. I wipe them away, embarrassed that he elicited a response like that. He leans over to kiss my damp cheeks, completely unsurprised by my wave of unexpected emotion. I know for sure in that moment, if I didn't know it before, that Smith was right not to sleep with me at his house that day. This was clearly what he needed and giving it to him brought me far more pleasure than I thought possible.

I glance over at Jax, curious now about him, even though I can barely feel my limbs right now. His eyebrows raise.

"You need a break," he says.

"I don't need a break," I blurt out, not at all interested in missing whatever is supposed to happen next.

"I don't think you can take anymore right now." He shakes his head. He doesn't seem disappointed when he says it, just a little resigned. There's supposed to be more. I can tell. And I want it all. Everything the two of them have to give me.

"Jax," his name rolls off my lips in a plea.

His expression falters. He might act so tough, but he's not immune to feelings. And goddamn, are there a lot of feelings in this room right now.

Caving to me, he climbs off the bed and offers me a hand. As I stand up next to him, leaning into him for balance, he offers Smith a hand to help him up, too. I don't know why, but apparently Smith does, because he shucks his used condom in the wastebasket by the bed and then takes the seat that Jax vacated before. Jax pushes me closer, his hand on the back of my neck as he has me stand directly in front of Smith's seated form.

"Put your hands on his knees," he tells me. *This is crazy.* But I do what he says.

Smith reaches for me, tucking my hair behind my

ear and then touching my cheek as I can feel Jax lining himself up against me. There's nothing in the world that could have prepared me for the moment he sinks into me.

There's nothing gentle about it this time like the first time. His hands grip my hips so hard I'm sure they'll be bruised later, but it's worth every wince of pain. He has to hold me that hard or I would go flying from the way he fucks me like he's punishing me. This is what I thought sex with Jax would be like, and it's every bit as delicious as having sex with him the first time was. I lose myself in all the sensations assaulting my senses. My hands on Smith's knees as Jax fucks me from behind. The gentle way Smith explores me from the front, but never enough to distract from what Jax is doing.

I thought it would be like taking turns having sex, but that's not how it actually feels. We're one unit. Each action blending into the next as the line between sex with Smith and sex with Jax blurs. When I'm overcome with yet another wave of pleasure, I cry out both their names, the syllables tangling until I'm not even sure either of them could tell what I cried out. My body feels weightless as Jax and Smith both help to hold me up until Jax finishes himself not long after.

As Jax pulls out of me, I sink down to the floor, my eyes on Smith as my legs give out on me. There's still one thing left that I want. I crawl between his legs, putting a hand on each of his legs as I watch mesmerized while he stokes himself.

"Can I?" I nod to his lap.

"Yeah," he chokes out.

I wrap my hand carefully around his, getting a feel for his rhythm for a moment before I'm brushing his hand away, wanting to touch him all by myself. I've never considered that I could be brazen in the bedroom, but damn if this day isn't bringing it out in me.

I glance up at him as I lower my head, our eyes locked as I sink my mouth down over the length of him. He groans, throwing his head back and breaking our eye contact. His hands find the back of my head and tangle into my hair, which I know must be a wreck by now.

As I start to bob my head, I can see Jax move closer from the corner of my eye. With a little extra effort, I can see enough of him to see that he's stroking himself as he watches me. His eyes are hooded as the sound of his groan joins Smith's. *Fuck, why is that so hot?*

I've never considered myself that big a fan of doing this, but there's something so unexplainably sexy about doing it knowing Jax is watching. That he's touching himself to this. It turns me on, knowing I'm pleasing them both like this.

Maybe Smith is onto something. There are serious perks to being three in a room.

It isn't long before Smith's warning me that he's

almost there. I pull back just in time as Jax tosses him a towel. *He was prepared.* Jax offers me a hand to stand again as Smith cleans himself up.

I'm not expecting it, but Jax pulls me up against his chest and kisses me long and hard. And holy hell, I've never imagined anything like how hot it could be to have a guy kiss me moments after I've had my mouth around another guy's dick.

Hours later, as the three of us lay tangled in a pile of limbs on the bed, each of us still only partially dressed, I'm struck by how truly full my heart feels. I might have decided to do this for Smith, but it turns out the person I really needed to do it for was me. I've been hanging on to these lingering fears that my dating arrangement with my guys isn't really okay, but I can't feel that way anymore after what just happened. How could anything ever be considered a mistake when it feels that good and that right? There's no going back now, not ever.

24

Sadie and Salma declare a girls' day after finding out what happened with Jax, Smith, and me. They want details, but I only give them little snippets, keeping most of it to myself. I don't think I could explain it all if I even tried.

We're set up in Sadie's room after she made her brother leave the house for the day. *"Don't act like you can be under the same roof as Jules and actually stay away,"* she'd told him when he tried to protest. So now he's off doing something with Patrick for the day while the girls pepper me with every awkward, probing question they can come up with. It's not just the sex they want to know about either. They want to know all the details they've missed out on since this whole thing started.

I want to be annoyed at the overabundance of questions, but a part of me is just relieved that Sadie is comfortable talking about it. After my visit with her at Banner-Hill, I really wasn't sure she'd ever accept this. I tell her as much.

"I should never have said what I did. I realized that after I saw this whole love triangle thing play out while I was there. The three of them just kept ending up hurt, and I couldn't help but think their problems would be solved if they'd just come to the same conclusion you have—that sometimes it's not about choosing." She sends me an apologetic smile.

I've forgiven her already, but it's nice to be reminded that there's no bad blood between us. We've finally started figuring things out, Sadie, Salma, and I settling into a friendship between the three of us that works. It turns out sharing isn't just for boyfriends. I got so caught up in my friendship with Salma for a while when Sadie was so out of sorts that when Sadie got back, it was hard to figure out how to make my friendships work. I don't know why I acted like the three of us couldn't be one cohesive unit. Now that they've gotten to know each other, I think Salma and Sadie are just as close to each other as I am to either of them.

"You know, there's been a lot of talk around school. People are starting to get curious. I'm willing to bet by Winter Break you're not the only sharing relationship at school. I'm sure everyone's parents are going to flip out once they realize it," Salma muses.

I cringe. "Yeah, I don't really envy dealing with that issue myself honestly." I'm lucky, I guess, that

Pearl's sickness allowed her to open up enough with me to cast her approval over my unorthodox relationship. I can't imagine how hard it's going to be if or when the whole thing comes up with the guys' parents. I don't imagine most of them are going to be nearly as understanding. The ones I've met all like me well enough now, but it's probably going to be a different story when they find out I'm carrying on relationships with three other guys.

I don't know, it's a problem for another day. I still maintain that my relationships aren't nearly as problematic as a lot of the shit that goes down here. I'm sure I'll make that argument when the time comes.

"Hey, I'm gonna go refill our drinks. Be right back," Sadie tells us as she stands up to take our drink tray back to the kitchen. She had mocktails made for us since none of us are drinking.

Once Sadie is gone, Salma turns to me. I can tell she's going to bring up her brother even before she does it, solely because the expression on her face is so sour. "I know I've apologized a gazillion times already, but I still feel like it hasn't been enough."

"Salma." I shake my head. "It wasn't your fault. People have to be responsible for their own shit, which means you don't have to take responsibility for your brother."

"I know," she groans, "but I just feel like I should have seen it. The obsession. The way he kept asking about you and getting pushier and pushier about it. You're so likable, it's easy to not be surprised when guys like you. But I should have seen that this was something different."

She's been saying more or less the same thing ever since that shit with her brother happened. Apparently, Salma's parents had neglected to let her in on some of the details of her brother being home instead of going back to college this fall. He assaulted a girl in the spring and got kicked out. Their parents decided the thing with me was the last straw. Unlike some parents in Patience, they decided to be proactive instead of sweeping things under the rug. I only had to make one statement to the police, at their parents' request, and now he's sitting in jail probably for the foreseeable future. Whatever plea deal he'd made after the first assault was voided after his second attempt.

The whole thing is so fucked up, and I've been forced to sit down with Dr. Peterson a few times because of it. Since the whole freaking school knows what happened. Not that it matters, I'm always careful not to say much to him. I've got plenty of people in my life to talk to—I have no interest in confiding in him.

I'm okay, despite how close I came to being seriously hurt. It's so easy to get caught up in second-guessing myself, wondering if I would have been safe if I'd just done some things differently. But then I remember that in the moment, I was able to save myself, and that makes me feel stronger than I think I ever have. The world is a scary place, but it means something to know I'm not helpless.

"Sometimes the people closest to us are the ones hardest to see clearly," I tell Salma just as my phone starts to ring. I glance at the caller ID, surprised to see Jan's name. I haven't been gone that long. A wave of dread crashes into me as I answer, "Hello?"

"Juliet?" I hear it in Jan's voice before she says the words. "You need to come home."

I'm up on my feet, moving across the room even before Salma can ask what's happening. She follows me out of the room, grabbing Sadie on her way back from the kitchen as I head for the front door. They figure out what's happening pretty easily as I start sprinting the distance from the Harringtons' to Lexington Estate. They aren't far behind me, but when we reach the house they pause outside the sitting room.

"We'll wait out here, in case you need us," Sadie tells me quietly.

My heart thumps painfully in my chest, my ribs feeling like they're contracting as I step into the room. Jan's face is full of sympathy as I collapse into her arms at the sight of Pearl struggling to breathe. She didn't want a million machines, so there's nothing forcing her to stay alive any longer than her body decides to be.

Jan hugs me for a long moment before pulling away and telling me, "I'll wait with your friends. You should have this time with your aunt." I nod, even though the words barely reach my brain.

I feel like I'm wading through water with the effort it takes to cross the room to the chair by Pearl's bed. I take her hand, trying not to shudder at how cold her hand feels.

"I'm glad you're home, my girl," Pearl says, surprising me. I can tell she doesn't just mean that I'm home right now. She means it in the bigger sense, that I came home to Patience last year, and home to her. Her eyes don't open, but her words are clearer than they've been in months. *Maybe it's not as bad as Jan thinks.* "Tell me what you'll do when I'm gone."

"No," I whisper, shaking my head. I don't want to think about that, much less acknowledge it out loud. We've had much longer together than anyone predicted, but I'm still not ready. It hasn't been enough time—it could never be enough time.

Tears roll over my cheeks as I grasp her hand tighter. Her fingers lightly squeeze back with what I imagine is all the strength she has left.

"You'll take care of the estate?" *She's really going to make me do this with her.*

"This is home," I somehow manage to choke out. "I'll always take care of it."

"Good." One of her fingers strokes the inside of my wrist. "And fill this place with babies, Juliet. This place deserves babies. I don't care if you have them with eight different men, just make sure you have them." She pauses for a quick wheeze. "Patience will get over it. They always do."

I can't help but laugh even as tears stream harder down my face. It's such a weird thing for her to be fixated on right now, but I guess I get it. It's been a long time since this house was a home full of life, and she just wants to know that I'll fix that. That I won't let the Lexington line end with me.

"I guess I'll have to hire a lot of nannies," I tell her, wanting things to be lighter. Wanting to not think about how the minutes are ticking down. How every minute that passes is one less I have left with her.

She falls into silence for several minutes and I lay my head down on the bed next to her as I keep hold of her hand. I don't even bother to conceal my sobbing. It hurts too bad to do anything but let it out. There are too many questions left unanswered and too many things we haven't done together. I should have taken an interest in Pearl's garden. Or asked her more about my father.

"Juliet." I raise my head and Pearl's eyes are open this time. She reaches out as if to pat me over my heart, but her hand wavers and misses. Her fingers accidentally brush the key around my neck, instead, sending it swinging on its chain. She blinks and then her eyes close again as she whispers, "You have everything you need right here."

And those are the last words she ever says.

25

"We made it work the best we could," the funeral director tells me apologetically.

I'm biting down hard on my bottom lip, and I can tell from the gentle way he talks that he's worried I'm going to start crying. I don't have the heart to tell him I'm trying not to fucking laugh. The casket looks absolutely ridiculous. White fabric is sticking out all over the place and I'm not honestly sure how they're going to get it closed. On such a sad day, it's nice to have something so outrageous to focus on. I wonder if Pearl anticipated that when she asked me for this.

"Put me in the one thing I never got to wear, Juliet. A wedding dress. Something very frilly that no one will expect. The bigger the better." Even though it was a request she made while not totally all there, it was something I still decided to honor.

And now, as I watch the funeral director panic

over how sloppy it looks, I know it was so, so worth the heartache of picking out a wedding dress for a woman who never got to actually wear one. I hand-picked it, too, refusing to let anyone take care of it for me when they offered. It was too personal, choosing Pearl's last outfit. I let other people help choose things like flowers and music. Neema was particularly helpful, though I hope the unannounced visits will stop now. There's something deeply horrifying about being interrupted in the middle of kissing one boyfriend when your other boyfriend's mom rings your doorbell.

At this point, I know she has to expect something is up. The estate has been a revolving door of boys every time she's shown up. Luckily, she's chosen not to say anything, but I'm not sure if that courtesy will extend past the funeral.

"Jules? People are starting to get here." I turn to see Sadie standing in the doorway.

I grimace as I look at the length of her dress. It was mine. I don't know what I was thinking when I bought it, but when I showed up here for the funeral, I pretty much immediately realized it was too short. It made me feel too exposed, which is the last thing I want today. And Sadie, who I will never again doubt my friendship with, for real this time—traded me dresses with absolutely zero hesitation. So now I'm in a perfectly respectable black dress while Sadie wears my slightly slutty one. That's true friendship.

"I'm coming," I tell her, taking one last deep

breath to avoid the laughter still threatening to come at any moment. I almost can't help myself, but I know if I start laughing there's a good chance I'll end up breaking into hysterics. There's a finer line between laughing and crying than you would think. I've learned that the hard way over the past few days.

My breath catches when I give the funeral director permission to open the doors and let other people in. My time of grieving alone has ended. I know there are other people that want to say good-bye, and even more people that I'm sure will show up just to be supportive. Pearl wasn't the friendliest lady, but she was a staple of this town.

I greet everyone individually, even though it pains me to do. There's quite the crowd, even more so than I expected, but I grit my teeth and bear it until the line finally starts to dwindle. My guys bring up the rear, having patiently waited despite how much I'm sure it's killing them to keep their distance. I had to tell them to back off a little this morning because they were suffocating me. I think it made them nervous, but I only needed space to be alone with my thoughts and the few memories of Pearl I have that I've been desperately clinging to.

I hug each of them, kissing them on their cheeks even though I'd rather be kissing them all properly. This isn't the time and place for coming out to the whole town though. I'm pretty sure most of the adults around here aren't privy to the teenage gossip, otherwise they'd all already know about our arrangement—and it's clear that's not the case. Not yet anyway.

I shoo the guys away when they try to linger, telling them to keep Sadie and Salma company while I finish my funeral hosting duties. I'll never make it through this if I start leaning on them. I need to stand on my own two feet in order to keep it together.

"Room for one more?" a voice asks just as I start to turn, thinking that's the last of the guests. I freeze, slowly pivoting back to face the open doorway. His hands are deep in his pockets as he gives me a sheepish look. His hair is longer than it was last year.

"Jake?" My voice cracks as I say his name. I wonder if I might need to ask for a casket of my own as my heart goes still in my chest. I rub one eye, almost certain that I'm hallucinating or something. Maybe the sleepless nights are finally catching up to me.

But then he's crushing me in a hug and I know it's real. I sink into his familiar arms, fisting the front of his shirt like I'm afraid he might turn and just leave at any moment. I never expected him to show up here. I don't know how he even knew. I raise my head a little so I can ask him.

"Your friend reached out to me. Or, your more than a friend, I guess." I follow his eyes as he looks over and finds Smith hanging back, keeping an eye on our interaction. "That guy does not like me much, though, does he?

"I think you might be the only person I've ever seen him actively dislike," I admit. *Besides Kareem*, I think to myself, but I'm not about to explain any of that to Jake right now. Not when he's finally come back to me—albeit under the worst of circumstances.

Jake squeezes me tighter. "I was really sorry to hear about your aunt. I thought about calling but I kept picturing you not answering or hanging up on me and I figured I needed to come in person, instead. Not as easy to turn me away if I'm actually standing in front of you, right?" He lets out a nervous half-laugh. I want to remind him that he's the one that walked away, not me. I spent months trying to get a response from him and got radio silence instead. But that's something we can talk about later. He's here now.

As if reading my mind, he tells me, "I'm not in any hurry to leave, okay? There will be plenty of time to talk later."

I nod just as the funeral director interrupts us to ask if I'm ready to start. I skipped out on the tradition of a visitation, trying to limit my interactions today, so we're going right to the actual funeral. I tell him I'm ready, even though I'm not so sure I feel like I am. Jake puts an arm around me, hugging me close to his side as he lets me draw strength from him. I was wrong. I do want to lean on someone. Several someone's, in fact.

I catch Smith's eyes and then gesture towards the

front. He jumps right into motion, talking quietly to each of the guys and sending them towards the front rows of the room. "Will you sit with us?" I ask, pointing out where the guys are situating themselves in two rows, leaving a clear spot for Jake and I to join them.

I see the wary way he looks the group over, and I wonder if Smith gave him any heads up about our situation. If not, we're going to be having a very uncomfortable conversation later.

"Of course, whatever you want." Jake walks with me up through the center of everyone to take our seats. I sit between him and Patrick, with Ace, Jax, and Smith in the row right behind us. I'm surrounded by love right now, I can feel it radiating off of them in waves. My guys have done everything they can to make this all bearable for me. I don't know how I would have done it without them. And now Jake is here too, and I feel complete in a way I never expected to. Especially not as I'm being forced to say goodbye.

As the minister Neema hired starts to deliver the eulogy, I let out a long, shuddering breath. I feel like I'm going to cry, but then nothing comes out of me. Almost as if I've finally cried myself out. My shoulders still shake with emotion, though.

Ace leans forward to put a comforting hand on my shoulder. He whispers to me, "You're okay, J. We've got you."

I nod, sniffling as the service drags on. I'm not

hearing any of it, so I'm not bothered when Jake leans over to talk quietly into my ear.

"J," he repeats Ace's nickname for me quietly. "I like that."

"You do?"

"Yeah. Because it's a name for who you really are. Not the Jessica Brown I grew up with anymore, but also not quite the Juliet Lexington that you were born to be. Calling you J, it's like... acknowledging that you're something in between."

I look at him, eyebrows raised as I realize he's put into words exactly the feeling I've had since arriving in Patience and learning who I really am. I'm perpetually stuck between two worlds, and learning to be the person in the middle. Because he's right, I'm not quite either of those people, but I'm also both. And I don't regret that for a second, because it led me here, to the saddest moment of my entire life as I say goodbye to a woman I learned to admire and respect, but surrounded by people that I love and am loved by. I don't know how anyone could ever ask for more than that.

26

They end up not being able to get the casket to close. The funeral director is horrified, even as the guys snicker around me. In the end, the guys help me take the train off the dress before the poor man pops a blood vessel. Her dress is still beautiful even without it, and in a way, I get to feel like I'm taking a small part of her home with me. A memory of our last months together, as chaotic and bizarre as they were.

The guys all come to the house, trailing behind Jake and I when I choose to ride with him in his brother's truck. "I've been driving a motorcycle at home," he admits, "But I traded with Brandon for now because there was no way in hell I wanted you on the back of that thing on the off chance you let me actually stay."

It's sweet, knowing he considered that, even

without the promise of this working out in his favor. Jake knows me though. I've always been a bit of a sucker with a tendency to forgive long past the point that I probably should. I don't know though, that's seemed to work out in my favor so far, if the five hot boys escorting me home have anything to say about it.

When we get to Lexington Estate, everyone stays to eat dinner with me, but after that I tell my guys they've got to go. There are a lot of protests all around, but I need time to talk to Jake alone. There's a lot we have to discuss and I don't want the guys butting in or creating problems by being overprotective. Plus, I can see the way Jake treads carefully around group conversation, like he's trying to figure out the dynamic of our group and he's worried about stepping on someone's toes. I need to tell him what's going on, and then if he leaves because of it, then so be it.

I love Jake. I've always loved Jake. But I'm not going to let anyone stop me from doing what makes me happy—not even him.

I walk them outside to say goodbye so that I don't have to do it under Jake's watchful stare. I want a proper goodbye since I won't see them again tonight. I'm sure they'll be back tomorrow, but right now that still feels like a whole lifetime away.

No one says a word when I kiss each of them goodbye. This isn't a habit of ours, because it's easier and more natural not to regularly be taking turns with them. But this is a special occasion, so *fuck it*. They get into their cars and leave as I watch them go, taking one last deep breath of the outside air before I brace myself to go face Jake.

He's waiting just inside the door for me, and I get the distinct feeling he saw me out there with them. His eyes glance briefly at the front window before back to me, only confirming my suspicion. It's not the first thing I want to talk about though.

"Why did you give my phone number to Lynne?"

His face goes red as he looks anywhere but at me. "It was fucked up, J. I was so mad, and there she was showing up everywhere I looked, reminding me you were gone. I wanted her to leave me alone, to just stop reminding me what I'd lost. So I gave her your info so she'd stop coming to find me."

"I went to see her," I admit, still turning Jake's words over in my head.

His eyebrows shoot up in surprise. "You did?"

I nod. "She was really messed up. She said some things… I'll tell you later. Anyway, it was actually good closure, maybe. I got some answers I needed because of that. So even though it still was really fucked up, yes, I'm not that mad about it anymore." It's something that I realized while sitting through the funeral. I couldn't find a single bone in my body that was still holding onto any anger.

"You've always been sweet. Sweeter than anyone deserves really." He starts to reach for me but then stops himself. "Out there, you…" He can't seem to find the words.

"I love them, Jake." I push out a long breath, wondering how I could ever begin to explain all that's happened in his absence. "My heart is full in Patience in a way it never was before. And we make it work. No one ever asks me to choose."

I'm not sure he really gets it, but he nods slowly anyway. "I wasn't sure coming back here if I could handle it. Seeing you with someone else again. It was pretty clear even over the phone that Smith really cared about you though, so I told myself to be okay with that. And as long as you were being taken care of, I needed to be able to live with the fact that it hadn't ended up being you and me."

"I—"

"No, let me finish." He doesn't say it to be mean. He just seems overwhelmed by the words falling off his lips. "I thought the hardest thing was going to be seeing you with someone else, but even seeing you with all four of them, it's still a hell of a lot less hard to stomach than not having you at all."

A silence falls between us as I study him, noting how genuine he looks about that. I expected a lot more pushback, but I can tell he means what he's saying. Jake's always wanted me to be happy, and he's not going to stop wanting that now just because my happiness looks different from what he expected.

"I love you," I tell him honestly. Maybe I

shouldn't be saying it, maybe it will only lead to more hurt, but I can't hold the words in. Not when I know how precious the time we have left is with the people we love.

"I love you, too, J." He puts his arms around me, and I can hear his heartbeat racing as I lay my head against his chest. "I just don't know what that means now," he admits softly.

My first instinct is to comfort him, to tell him we'll figure it out, but I'm in no position to promise him that right now. I've already torn my little love group apart by making decisions by myself. I'm not going to do that this time. I have to learn from my mistakes. So, I don't say anything, just holding him for a long time so that I don't make the mistake of making any empty promises. Nothing has to be decided today. Jake's not going anywhere.

We stay like that for a long time before I admit that I'm exhausted. "I probably don't have any right to ask this…" I trail off.

"You can ask me for anything." Jake pulls back so he can look at me.

"Can you stay in my room tonight?" I second-guess my request when his face falls. "You really don't have to. There's a billion guest rooms here. You can stay in one of those."

"God, no. As much as I absolutely don't deserve it, I want nothing more than to stay in your room with you. But is that… Is that crossing a line with the guys you're seeing? Smith did me a favor calling for me to come here, I don't want to show up and piss everybody off just to end up being shut out. I don't ever want to go that long without talking to you again."

There's real concern on his face. It's actually sweet, that he's being considerate of my relationships even if he doesn't necessarily understand them yet. We're on the same page too, because I don't want to do anything to make the guys distrust Jake either. I want them to like him. I want to know that no one's going to be up in arms about me being friends with him again.

"What if we stay down here in the guest room instead?" I suggest.

He frowns. "Is that, uh, different somehow?"

"Yeah." I nod. "Sleeping in the same bed in a guest room feels way less intimate than sharing my bed in my actual bedroom." I'm not sure if the logic checks out, but I think I'd do just about anything to convince him now. I don't want to sleep alone in this big, empty house.

"Okay," he caves, just like I hoped he would.

We climb into the guest bed on the main floor fully clothed. My borrowed dress rides slightly up my legs but it's still long enough to cover me. It's going to be wrinkled as hell in the morning. I make a mental note to have it professionally dry-cleaned before giving it back.

I glance at Jake, hating the way he lays stiff on the opposite side of the bed. He feels me looking at him and turns his head to meet my eyes. With a soft sigh, he holds an arm out to me. "C'mon, then."

My heart soars as I scoot across the bed and curl up against him. There's nothing suggestive about it, it's just a comfort that I need. I rest my head in the crook of his shoulder as we fall into easy conversation, talking about all the things we missed in each other's lives. I don't know how long we talk before I fall asleep, but it feels like no time has passed at all before my eyes are opening, blinking against the morning sun that streams in through the window.

I'm still nestled up next to Jake, but he's a heavy sleeper so I manage to get out of bed without waking him. Yesterday was a lot. If he's able to sleep, I want to let him. Plus, I know how fucking comfortable these beds feel the first time sleeping on one after sleeping on shit mattresses in Nikon Park all our lives.

The house is so quiet and calm that I don't get any warning about the sight that greets me when I step into the kitchen. Four grumpy guys are sitting around the island, all turning to stare at me as I enter with soft footsteps. "Good morning?" I say hesitantly. I know for sure I locked the doors last night, but I don't think I even want know how they got in here this morning. No one returns my greeting and I feel my heart start to sink.

"We saw you in bed with him," Ace explains, dropping his head so that he's not looking at me as he says it. Shit. If Ace is upset with me, then I really know it's bad.

I tuck my hair behind my ears, trying to buy myself a minute. I didn't expect to be facing this first thing when I woke up. "Nothing happened," I tell them. "All we did was talk and sleep." Jax snorts like he doesn't believe that at all, but he falls silent when Smith shoots him a sharp look.

Jake chooses that moment to make his appearance, his bedhead probably not the best look considering the topic of conversation. "Hey," he says, but then stops short in the doorway when he realizes the mood in here is not great. "Fuck," he mutters. This was exactly what he was telling me last night that he didn't want.

"Can we just—" I'm about to ask if we can just not make such a big deal about this but I'm interrupted by the sound of knocking on the front door.

I'm not actually sure if I'm grateful for the interruption or not, but I storm right out of the room anyway. I feel guilty now for sleeping in the same bed as Jake, which isn't fair because it's probably the only reason I was able to get any sleep at all. I jerk the front door open admittedly harder than I should. There's a carrier on the other side of the door, his eyebrows rising as he shoots an unimpressed look my way.

"Juliet Lexington?" I confirm it's me and then sign the clipboard he holds out. In a deadpan voice, he says, "this is for you," and thrusts a sealed yellow envelope out at me.

I mumble a thank you as I close the door, already turning to go back to the kitchen. I'm not so sure I should be leaving Jake alone with the other guys for any length of time. But when I return, things seem fairly calm. Jake is leaning on the island, eyes turning to me expectantly as I walk in.

"Everything okay?" he asks.

"Just a delivery," I shrug, working my finger under the seal to open it. I pull the paperwork out and spread it out over the island. A wave of emotion coasts over me, forcing me to close my eyes as I realize what this is. I play with the key on my necklace, a nervous habit I seemed to have picked up these last few days. When I open my eyes again, the guys are all staring at me with worried looks.

It's the final copies of everything, my ownership of the entire Lexington legacy, all tidied up into one long document confirming everything I now own. Sealed and delivered, courtesy of Grant Harrington. I hate that he didn't give me more time. I glance over some of the papers, overwhelmed by all the information. I'm not even sure what to do with all of it. There are instructions towards the back telling me how to get access to each of the properties, so that's something at least.

I skim over them, knowing I'm without a doubt going to have to find help to wade through all of this. Something on the paper catches my eye. I put my finger on the page, reading the same spot over and over again.

"What's wrong?" Patrick asks as the guys all seem to pick up on my distress.

I look up at them as I rip my necklace off and throw the key down on the island. "I know where Hollis' treasure is."

Made in the USA
Columbia, SC
11 August 2021